"Win had an idea of playing around with the Don Quixote story but turning it upside down, making the older character useless and the young one daring. We brainstormed, staying away from "The Impossible Dream," and he turned it into one of the great comic reads about the West." — *Dale Wasserman, author of Man of La Mancha*

"The two main characters get into amazing scrapes from wrestling bears, to falling in love with off-limits women in Santa Fe, a Crow woman warrior, and the porcelain-faced daughter of a trader. A great read of two truly American characters!" — *Tony Hillerman*

"Blevins 'Silk and Shakespeare' brims with good-natured fun!" — *Publisher's Weekly*

"A romp! The Misadventures of Silk and Shakespeare is a fun house and roller-coaster ride in one. Blevins's background is solid—he knows the mountain man life—but the fun here is the mismatched main characters. Thanks to Shakespeare's talent for getting them into trouble, they have a wild time of it, and so does the reader. — *Meg Mathews, Boston, USA*

THE MISADVENTURES OF

Silk and Shakespeare

WIN BLEVINS

The Misadventures of Silk and Shakespeare
Copyright© 2013 by Win Blevins
Blevins, Winfred.
The misadventures of silk and shakespeare / Win Blevins
1. Frontier America—Fiction. 2. Indians of North America—
Fiction.
Published in the United States of America

ISBN-13: 9780692203811
ISBN-10: 0692203818

CONTENTS

ACKNOWLEDGMENTS

My son Adam, by word and deed, inspired lots of this novel. His spirit seems to me, genie-like, to live in every page. To him my thanks and my love. Thanks also to my friend Murphy Fox, who answered many questions about Indian customs and Montana topography.

His fantasy was filled with those things that he read, of enchantments, quarrels, battles, challenges, wounds, wooings, loves, tempests, and other impossible follies.
—Miguel de Cervantes

1

Exit, pursued by a bear

—The Winter's Tale, III.iii

Tal rummaged in his shot pouch. Somewhere underneath all these lead balls and greasy patches…

Rosie stopped. She didn't like the hard work of carrying this boy uphill anyway, so when he dropped the reins like that, she just stopped. And moon-eyed him sideways.

"Rosie, old girl, old mulie," Tal piped, like it was the top of the finest morning in the Garden of Eden, "we need a flag to march under, and I've got one here somewhere." He spilled some patches onto the rough track, a game trail he was following up into these Black Hills. So he swung down and set his rifle on the ground and started emptying his shot pouch—patch knife, cut patches, ticking greased with bear lard, spare ticking, .50-caliber lead balls, ball-starter, ball-puller, ball-maker, a chunk of raw lead the size of his hand, flints, a spare fire steel, a folding knife, a handful of fur from the underside of a beaver—a pack-rat clutter.

Once his aunt had called out to him, as he was headed for the woods, that good woodsmen were prepared for all eventualities—called out in the condescending way she saved for children. Miffed, he'd dumped it all on the drawing-room floor to show Aunt Pitty what preparation meant. She'd gotten one whiff of the stale bear grease and strutted off swinging her full skirts and threatening to faint.

Well, Aunt Pitty, it's one American boy's complete, do-it-all, up-to-date survival kit. Of course that was two years ago, when he was still a boy, and a resident of civil-eye-zation.

At last he remembered—he'd used it for a bookmark. So Tal stuffed a hand into the blankets tied behind the saddle (Rosie fidgeted and flicked her mule ears) and brought out his treasured copy of Miss Jane Porter's *Scottish Chiefs*. Noting the page, he took out the bookmark, bent over his old Lancaster rifle, and tied it to the wiping stick.

A silk handkerchief, orange and blue. The color of flame bordered by the color of sky. His blazon, the armorial bearing of the house of Jones.

He repacked, swung into his saddle, touched his heels to Rosie's bony flanks, and started on up the ridge. He seated the battered rifle on the pommel and held it straight up in the air—the silk handkerchief near the muzzle, fluttering in the breeze, caught the morning sun handsomely. He pictured Robert the

Bruce, riding across the heath at the head of a thousand bloody-minded Scot patriots, flying the banner of his clan in so fresh a breeze, under so fine a morning sun.

And was not his present mission, to get meat for his hungry comrades, worthy as well? Tal meant one day to set down his Rocky Mountain adventures, his modern knight-errantry, in a book. He had a notebook, and though he seldom found time to write, he often thought as he rode how he would word something, imagined just how it would sound in the ears of his readers. He had his dedication already:

To my father, David Dylan Jones, who devoted his life to the pulpit and to poesy until the day he struck for freedom—and the mountains.

Tal reached up and scratched Rosie's gawky ears affectionately. She lowered her head to get the ears out of reach.

At noon Tal decided to have a good look around and figure out just where he was. He let Rosie graze in a nice glade while he climbed a boulder and turned his spyglass every direction.

To the northeast lay the north fork of the Platte River. Though he couldn't see it clearly through the dust and haze, he could make out the dark line of cottonwoods that marked its banks. Running the glass along the wide plain, he couldn't pick up any sign of his brigade, the forty fur trappers he'd left Taos with three weeks ago. Oh well, he knew where to find them—back to the river and make tracks for the Shining Mountains, where the wily beaver swims, and dusky maidens dwell. He lined the glass along the south side of the river again. Strange there should be no sign of them. Oh well.

He turned the glass toward the summits of these mountains, the Black Hills, the trappers called them. Prime hunting country, just like the other Black Hills up by the Cheyenne River. Tal made little maps of such things in his notebook, to get the vast plains and great rivers and the Shining Mountains in his head. So far these Black Hills were August dry, parched and hot in the lower reaches. The game would be up high, feeding on the little grasses made green by the high, cold alpine streams.

That was why Tal had sneaked off here. Cap'n Fitzpatrick was in a hurry—time for rendezvous was already past—and he wouldn't stop to make meat. The men were tired of Mexican beans and jerky. Everyone wanted fresh roasts and steaks, but Fitzpatrick only smiled coolly at their complaints and said, "Forty miles tomorrow." So Tal would surprise them with elk. The carcass would get to ride while Tal hoofed it into camp, triumphant.

He glanced at his Lancaster by his side, and at Rosie in the glade. One gift from his dad was being able to shoot—Tal could drive a pine needle or trim your mustache with a lead ball. Yes, a talent for marksmanship, a disdain for cussing, and the gift of song were his legacy from David Dylan Jones.

He put the glass back to his eye and started scouting the meadows for fat does.

And saw a man. A big man. A gargantuan man. A man tall enough to stand higher than the horse he was leading. A man with legs that were tree trunks, a chest like an ale keg. A bear of a man, and hairy as Old Ephraim—Tal adjusted the focus—his brown mane to his shoulders, his beard clear up to his cheek bones and down to his belly. Tal put the glass down and spied the fellow with the naked eye. He was not even two hundred yards away. Strange he hadn't heard Tal coming.

The hairy fellow was stalking something. Had to be. He was creeping, near as a man that size could creep.

Then Tal saw it. About fifty yards behind Big Hairy was a bear. Tal put the glass on it. A grizzly bear. The great silvertip. Old Ephraim himself.

And the beast was watching Big Hairy. Clear as day, the bear would peer out from around a clump of bushes and spot Hairy, move back, and rear up and look over the bushes at the man. The bear was stalking the man, the hunted stalking the hunter.

Tal considered. Should he yell, and warn Hairy? Might scare Old Ephraim, and the beast was as likely to attack as run off. Should Tal ride down there? Rosie wouldn't stand for it. Should he shoot the bear? At this range a lead ball would only annoy the animal.

What would Tal want done, in Hairy's place? Heck, Tal would want to be left alone. If Hairy was hunting the bear, best to handle it himself. What honor would there be in having the quarry run off by a stranger? What valor in a quest ended by an outsider? No, if he were Hairy, Tal would brook no interference. He settled down to watch.

Hairy looked down, then studied the ground ahead along the lush grass, across a rivulet, and into some willows. He turned and patted his horse's neck, got a couple of things from his possible sack. He dropped the reins and took a moment to put on a hobble. Then he checked the priming on his gun and advanced stealthily toward the willows. He was holding something Tal couldn't make out in one hand, something dark.

At the bank of the rivulet Hairy sat down, laid his gun across his lap, and put the dark thing on his head. It was a hat, a hat—ye gods!—made from a bear head, and it covered him to the shoulders. Then he got down on all fours and sniffed the air. He sat and scratched at his shoulders, and sniffed his crotch, the way Tal had seen black bears do.

The griz was still watching from the bushes. Tal bet himself Old Ephraim thought Hairy was tetched.

Now Hairy stood up, in sort of an important way, like preachers do before communion. He raised his huge hands high into the air and danced a jig. He began to shake—hands and arms and head and belly and all quivering like crazy. And then he roared like griz, a huge and horrible sound such as Tal had never heard in his life.

Griz roared back.

Griz bounded out from behind that bush and rose high like Hairy and shook its paws and made an awful roar.

Hairy, picking up his gun, was peering into the willows with all his soul. For a long moment he froze in that position, unable to believe his ears. Then, theatrically, he slowly pivoted his head on his doubting shoulders and looked behind.

Old Ephraim, reared up and ready.

The two glared at each other. Griz roared. Hairy roared back. Tal didn't know which of them sounded more like a bear. They were jousting with lungs for lances.

It happened too fast.

Hairy was throwing his gun to his shoulder and griz was on all fours and charging and Tal hit the ground running forward and Hairy's shot shook the trees and the bear was almost on top of Hairy and Tal would never get there in time.

The bear ran over Hairy, but Hairy was off to one side and rolling and getting to his feet. The bear charged again. Out from under Hairy tumbled. He came up holding his pistol and kaboomed with it.

Griz rose on its hind legs. It roared as only a thousand pounds of angry can roar. Maybe neither shot hit home. Hairy jumped for his rifle. Griz didn't move. Hairy held the unloaded gun toward the bear. Tal had the crazy thought that Hairy was going to put Old

Ephraim through some dance steps. Tal was only half-way there and his chest was already hurting.

Man and bear faced other, looked each other over. Hairy circled like a boxer. Griz just stood, imposingly still. Finally Hairy slipped the wiping stick off the barrel. And with a nutty leap he closed and whacked the bear on the nose with the stick.

"Hiya-hi-hiya," shouted Hairy exuberantly.

Tal couldn't believe it. Sumbuck counted coup on a grizzly bear. Tal got to one knee and checked his priming powder. All gone. Tal started priming.

Griz just stood there, eyeing the man. And then, quick as a fish, moved.

Hairy swung the rifle and might have glanced the heavy barrel off the bear's head. They grappled. They rolled over. And over again. Tal thought he saw Hairy's hand rise and fall with a tomahawk. He watched them over his hind sight, but with the two of them wrestling, he couldn't risk a shot.

Then he saw griz's paws swat and Hairy hit the ground like a sack of grain. Tal had to try. He held on Old Ephraim's head and pulled.

Griz flinched. He faltered. He stumbled. He fell on Hairy.

Tal decided to reload, right now.

Hairy stirred. Pushed. Grunted. Humped. Wriggled free.

He looked down at the beast. Griz was still as stone.

Hairy shook his fists at the sky and lifted a cry into the burning air, a cry of bloodlust, of blood-letting, of life crowing over death. His hair flowed down his back and belly. Blood flowed from under his bear hat and down his face. He was as much beast as griz.

Seating his ball, Tal raised his thin, reedy voice as a chorus to Hairy's, a thin but avid cry of triumph.

Hairy looked at Tal. Looked at Griz's skull, which was caved in. Looked at Tal.

Priming again, Tal smiled foolishly at the beast-man.

Hairy searched on the ground for his tomahawk. Found it. Studied Tal. Glared at Tal. Stalked toward Tal, hawk raised.

Tal jumped up. As he started to run, the hawk whizzed past his ear. It made an ugly whup-whup sound through the air. It made Tal mad.

Tal whirled. Hairy was at full run and almost on him. In one motion Tal threw the rifle up and pulled the trigger. The world roared. Shattered into light. Went black.

2

O day and night, but this is wondrous strange!
                    —Hamlet, I.v

Light was seeping in, like water into a cellar. Tal moved, and noted that he felt sort of like himself. He blinked open and quickly shut. The daylight looked earthly enough. Then he realized what was wrong—he couldn't move his chest to breathe. And he remembered something about the bear and the man and...

Tal had shot Hairy. He wondered if Hairy was dead. Probably so. Tal's recollection was that the shot took Hairy in the face. He turned his head to the side a little (his neck still worked) and looked straight into the face of the bear—eyes dead and teeth gaping.

Whoa-a.

If Tal wasn't pinned but good, that scare would have taken him out from under. Now Tal could see the side of Hairy's huge head between the bear's teeth, and remembered the bear hat. It was a black bear hat, he could see now. It must have gotten turned somehow. The side of Hairy's head looked like a big wound, the long hair soaked with thickening blood.

Darn. Tal squirmed, got a little more breathing room. Didn't seem worth the effort to get out from under. Maybe he couldn't get out from under, and was headed for the Promised Land with Hairy. If so, he didn't want to think on it yet.

Poor Hairy. He looked so magnificent challenging griz with griz. Even if griz was the other direction, and Hairy was roaring at the willows.

Where the devil could Hairy have got that idea? Tal had seen every sort of white man trap every sort of animal—it was done with a combination of place-ment, disguise, and bait. Those ways were clever, but what Hairy did was grand. Tal had heard medicine men brought the buffalo herds within range of the arrow by dressing like buffalo and doing a dance. Maybe…

Well, what had Tal come west for but to see the wondrous and the rare? Now Hairy was dead and couldn't teach Tal the grizzly magic. Darn.

Tal looked sideways at Hairy's bloody, blown-up head.

It turned.

Hairy's face came into view. The mouth opened, the nose puckered, the eyes squinched. Lips and teeth quivered. It was a yawn, the most prodigious yawn Tal had ever been privileged to witness, espe-cially at such close range—a yawn worthy of the ugliest giant of yore. Hairy's features were gigantic anyway—nose like a butte, pores like caves, teeth like worn, cracked boulders. Hairy exhaled, and no dragon's breath could have been more foul, more rank, more putrid.

Tal poked the big carcass. He had to get out from under before he suffocated. Jabbed with his knees. Grabbed the big nose and twisted hard.

"Ow!" said Hairy, and popped his eyes open. He stared at Tal close range for a moment, sat up shaking his head.

"Thought I done you in," Hairy mumbled, fingering his nose gingerly.

"Thought I done you in," answered Tal.

"Hearing's funny," Hairy said. He shook his monstrous head. "Now let me recollect…" His voice was resonant, orotund, cavernous, the voice in which the burning bush instructed Moses. And it had British inflections. He was thinking, moving his fingers like he was counting, the black-bear muzzle bobbing up and down. One of the fingers had a hard, wrinkled nail, like a walnut shell.

Tal felt for his belt knife, just in case.

When Hairy had it straight in his mind, he said meekly, "You likely saved my life." He looked at Tal with sheepdog eyes in a black-bear head. "You likely saved my life. Griz had one up on me."

"Why'd you try to kill me?" said Tal. He needed whatever advantage he could get before Hairy figured out who shot him.

"Went into one of my crazies, I guess." He sounded meek. He twisted the bear head, and lifted it off. His huge, balding head was a mass of bleeding scratches, not counting the gunshot wound on the side. He looked mournfully at the bear head in his hands. "Bad medicine, I guess, to go for my griz wearing just a black bear. An insult, I guess."

He turned his head toward Tal. "I'm powerful grateful to you," he said resonantly. "Can't recollect anyone saved my life before." Gratitude dripped from him like blood.

"Let me help you with those cuts," Tal offered, embarrassed. He fished a pinch of that belly fur out of his shot pouch.

Hairy put his hands on his scalp, looked at the blood on them, got on his knees, and presented the top of his head to Tal. "Powerful grateful," he murmured, a murmur that would carry to the furthest peaks. "Reckon I owe you. This child surely does owe you."

Tal was daubing on the fur. It stopped the flow right off. He wished he could stanch Hairy's grateful, sheepdog glances. He turned the head sideways to inspect the gunshot wound, and get away from those eyes.

After a moment, Tal said, "You'd best not be so grateful. Seems I blew your ear off." That explained all the blood—nothing would bleed like an ear. Tal started in with the belly fur on the remaining stub of ear. He ought to wash it out, he knew, but he was worried about the amount of blood this fellow was losing—Hairy's patriarchal beard was getting crimson with it. The wounds could be washed later.

"Powerful grateful," murmured Hairy at a soft roar. "Eternally grateful."

"Doesn't your ear hurt?" said Tal, a little sharply.

"No," allowed Hairy, rubbing his nose. "But my nose hurts. Never woke up that way before." He flicked his glance up at Tal and back down. "Not meaning to be offensive," he said. "This child is powerful grateful to ye."

"All right," said Tal, "you'll live." In fact, Tal wasn't so sure—Hairy'd lost a lot of blood.

Tal got to his feet and offered his hand. "Tal Jones," he said, sticking out his hand.

Hairy was on his knees but he took the hand. "Ronald," he said.

Ronald. Giant Hairy—Hairy Giant—was Ronald. Hairy was struggling to his feet, and Tal nearly got pulled over.

When Hairy got onto two legs, like a human critter, Tal grasped how big he was. Not only tall but broad. And thick. To weigh him, you'd have to hang him, like beef.

Tal himself was slight in every way—not quite to middling height, reedy of build. People told him that his shock of buckeye-colored hair and green eyes were cute, especially in summer when his freckles set them off. They also told him he might grow some more. He hated both remarks—you didn't tell men such things, and Tal was a sixteen-year-old man.

"I own to the name my blessed parents gave me," said Hairy. "Ronald Dupree Smythe, rhyming with scythe." The huge voice made Tal feel like an aspen quaking in the breeze. "But I prefer the title given by my colleagues, my fellow hunters of the beaver. Shakespeare." Said with a glint of pride.

Shakespeare? "How come?" Tal didn't want to say the name. His recollection of the Bard of Avon was memorizing lines by sing-song and reciting them in chorus with his father.

The giant pondered Tal's expression, of voice and of face. "That will come when we're better acquainted," Hairy said, smiling down at Tal. "You may call me what you want for now."

Tal didn't think it would be Ronald or Shakespeare, but could he call the fellow Hairy? Hairy reached down for Tal's rifle, still lying on the ground.

"What's this?" the big man said. The gun looked like a wiping stick in his big hand. He fingered the orange and blue silk handkerchief.

"This dainty was the last thing I saw before you shot me," Hairy went on. "A flash of orange, and then a roar." He bared his boulder teeth, and clacked them once. "What a roar!" He shook his head, maybe clearing his ears, then challenged Tal with a hard eye. "How come you got an orange silk hanky tied on?"

Tal flushed, and flushed some more. "Well," he said, reaching for his rifle. "Well..." He covered his flag, his banner, with his hands.

Hairy nodded. He smiled a smile as wide and deep as a canyon. "Never you mind. Let's get that bear skinned out."

"By God," roared Hairy gently, "you have shot the grizzly bear. You slew the mighty silvertip—he of the sharp claw, the prodigious paw, and the powerful jaw. You are the conqueror of Old Ephraim, the beast that strikes terror into the heart of 'ary a mortal man." He grinned an immense grin at his little St. George.

Hairy, who had been carrying on in this exuberant manner for some time, started cutting thin slices of meat. The naked bear lay on the stretched-out hide, pathetically male, looking not at all like a thousand pounds of terror.

Tal was building a squaw fire nearby—he was hungry. Despite his aw-shucks gestures, he was not sufficiently embarrassed by Hairy's carrying on to get him to stop. After all, he had killed griz, hadn't he? And saved a man's life? With a single clean shot in desperate circumstances? A tale for his notebook, a brag for the book he meant to make of his adventures.

The old hands of the mountains had distinctive nicknames, Tal knew, names like Old Bill, Bad Hand, Blanket Chief, and Cut Face. Tal wondered if someone would name him Old One-Shot. He tried it on the tongue a little. Not bad. Old One-Shot. Or Man-in-a-Pinch. More Indian style—Man-in-a-Pinch. He didn't like it as well. Old One-Shot.

"Fire's about ready," Tal said.

Hairy slid a couple of bacon-thin slices onto skewers and handed one to Tal. "Make sure she's done, lad, make sure." Hairy eyed Tal. "You ain't slew bear before, have ye?"

Tal, keeping his eyes down, shook his head no.

Hairy put a shoulder roast into a pot of water and set it in the fire. "Well, great balls of fire," he said, "how many eighteen-year-old kids have gone against Old Ephraim and won?" He eyeballed Tal, who in fact was only sixteen and looked less than that, but didn't like to be called a lad, which sounded like kid.

Just who'd saved whose tail here, anyhow? "How come you were luring that bear with that, uh, was it a medicine dance?"

"That bear was big medicine, lad, big medicine." Hairy watched the bear grease make the fire spit for a moment.

"Let me tell you. I been hanging out with these 'Rapahoes up in North Park, living with them and all." He looked up at Tal. "You lived with Injuns much?" Tal shook his head.

"Hoss, it's good living. Good living. The women are whoo-ee!" Hairy eyed Tal, who nonchalantly took a bite off his slice.

"Well, this Red Horse, he's got a daughter I fancy. Name of Sweet Spring. This child wishes to drink deep of that girl, he does.

When birds do sing, hey ding-a-ding-ding, Sweet lovers love the spring."

Hairy orated these words musically, and glanced shyly at Tal, who was gape-mouthed. Hairy orated the words once more, even more musically.

"Red Horse, however, took no fancy to this child. Though this child had pleasured a severalty of the 'Rapahoe women, Red Horse thought him not man enough for Sweet Spring. So I set a course to show myself a Launcelot" (he broadened it to Lawnce-lot) "for Sweet Spring, and perhaps Red Horse's two younger daughters at the same time."

Hairy checked out Tal's reaction, but Tal was a study in indifference. He reached for another slice.

"Women have trouble keeping up with my appetites," Hairy explained softly. (This turned out to be one boast of Hairy's that could be verified.) "I could use three wives." Hairy skewered two slices.

"So I dreamed this griz. Dreamed him over and over, night after night. If I saw Sweet Spring in the evening, this child was sure to dream bear that night. Couldn't say for sure what sex my dream bear was, but it had a big silver ring around its neck."

He pointed at the skin on the ground with his skewer and grinned. The bear had a wide silver ring around its neck.

"This child had an idea. Conquer the mighty grizzly in fair and furious battle." He made this phrase ring. "Make griz medicine. Eat the hair of the bear. Tote the talon of the silvertip." He thumbed the necklace he was wearing, made of black-bear claws. "Give Red Horse a present of something griz. Give the robe to Sweet Spring for our bed. Big medicine." He pondered that. Tal did too, and turned red.

"So I took a sweat bath—you done a sweat bath?"

Tal mumbled no. Felt he hadn't done anything, being just a gosh darn lad.

"Wagh! That's where a child gets himself ready for something big. Like seeking a dream grizzly and slaying it and getting medicine from it.

"So I set out into these hills to find the holy grail of a griz." Hairy spread his arms to the sky. "And get a squaw for my connubial cave."

He chuckled, and his chuckle rolled like distant thunder. They both took more meat.

"Hoss, it was some. I cut sign. I tracked, and tracked. I could *smell* griz. Could *smell* it wasn't just some old bear but my dream bear, my medicine bear, the beast of the silver ring.

"Got a glimpse of him two days ago. Silver ring, right there, yea verily. Wagh!"

This last sound was a sharp bark, like the bark of a bear if bears could bark, beginning softly and throatily and growing to a pop like a bullwhip's. It made Tal jump.

"Waa-a-gh!" Hairy repeated, popping it with satisfaction.

"This morning I cut fresh sign. Stowed my pack horse. Closed in. Moved dainty-like, got real close."

Tal considered putting in that it was the bear that moved dainty-like and got real close, but thought better of it.

"Next, as you say, I did my medicine dance. How say? A coon imitates the animal he's hunting to be more like it, get in good with it, get close like a brother. Some such anyway."

Hairy's face suddenly dropped, like he'd changed from comic mask to tragic. He was a perfect pose of glumness.

"Well, hoss, you saw what happened after that. I missed." He stared at his stony knuckles. "You shot him and saved my skin."

Hairy whipped his skewer at the ground, where it stuck like a knife. They watched it quiver.

"Can't you make medicine of the griz anyhow?" Tal ventured.

"Ho-o-o-ss," said Hairy in an aggrieved tone. "That would be a dissembling." He pierced Tal with a reprimanding eye. "Dissembling. Besides, you toy with medicine like that and it will toy with you. Wagh!"

All the slices were gone. Hairy poked at the simmering roast with his knife and shook his head.

"Tell you what, though, tell you what. You conquered the mighty griz in fair and furious battle. *You* make medicine of him."

Well. Tal kept his face straight. Who-o-o-o-p-e-e-e-e! he shouted in his head.

3

but all in honour

—Othello, V.ii

Hairy showed Tal how to take the claws off—
big ones, the size of Tal's fingers. "Takes a lot
of griz to make a whole necklace," Hairy observed.
"And a lot of man to get a lot of griz." Just let the claws
lie in your possible sack, Hairy said, until the extra
skin dried and then peel it off.

"Lad," said Hairy, catching Tal in the act, "you
don't actual eat the hair of the bear. A man with
the ha'r of the b'ar in him—that's just a manner of
speaking." Tal spit the dry, gritty hairs into his hand.
He didn't think he could have swallowed them anyway.

Hairy skinned the head, a delicate job if you
wanted to use it for a hat. He handed Tal the skull.
"Hang the skull in front of your lodge," he advised,
"and use the jawbones for knife handles."

Hey—a knife handle. Tal started drying off a jaw-bone. Hairy was fingering the head skin. Made Tal think.

He lifted the head skin on the point of his knife and faced Hairy ceremoniously. "Friend Ronald the Hairy Giant," Tal said, "known to comrades as Shake-speare, as a token of my admiration for your bear-like courage, I hereby give you the head of this grizzly bear. May it protect your bare head from the enemy sun."

Hairy took it, his face tangled in feeling.

"Being as I shot heck out of your previous hat," added Tal, grinning.

Hairy extended one arm, made quick circles with the hand, and gave a deep bow. "True, this child tracked Old Silver Ring, didn't he?" He sat down, looking reflective.

In a few minutes he had the head on, and Tal had to look at him through those huge teeth.

They made camp right on the spot of the kill, a plenty good place, said Hairy.

"We've told the Injuns where we are with all those shots," Tal complained.

"Ah, lad," Hairy answered easily, "there be no Injuns about here. Not a red critter in these entire Black Hills—not this time of year."

So Tal dozed while Hairy collected Rosie and his pack horse. When Tal woke up, Hairy had a bigger fire going and more bear roast cooking. "Carry your spare rations here," Hairy roared, patting his huge belly, "and you'll allus have them handy.

"We'll get some deer for the brigade tomorrow," Hairy assured him. "Bloody hell, the boys shouldn't have to get by on dried meat, sure not. Them boosh-ways"—that was slang for brigade leaders—"they don't care nothing for the ordinary chap, they sure don't. Cap'n Fitzpatrick, he's no better than the others, sure not."

Hairy acted like, sure, Tal wanted and needed him for a partner. A youngster like you, his manner said, alone in these vasty mountains....Well, never you mind, lad, this hoss will help ye out. Seemed to Tal that things like this, unspoken things, were usually bigger than the ones that got spoken.

After lunch—Tal was twice as full as he thought he could be—Hairy got solicitous, or curious. He got Tal to tell how he came from St. Louis, and his father was a preacher man—"a bearer of Gospel," Hairy said sonorously.

"How come ye to choose the mountain life?" queried Hairy. "Was your fantasy filled with those things that you read"—this was in his recitation voice—"of enchantment, quarrels, battles, challenges, wounds, wooings, loves, tempests, and other impossible follies?"

Tal could have hugged him. These lines were among Tal's father's favorites—one of their most cheering ways of passing times was telling tales of the knight errantry of the great Don Quixote. Why, wasn't Rosie even named after Rosinante, Quixote's gallant, broken-down steed? "I asked ye, lad, what impossible folly led ye to the mountain life?"

Well, Tal had a repertory of inventions for that: How he'd been apprenticed to a blacksmith but run away from the beatings. How he was the black sheep of a musical family, not being able to carry a tune. How he'd stabbed a man in a fight over a girl, and had to flee the law.

Right now none of those entertaining lies pleased him. "Somep'n like that," Tal said meekly. "And I had to get shut of my aunt.

"Hairy," Tal started tentatively, "you met anybody named Jones in the mountains afore? My dad, he come out in '29."

Hairy gave him a shrewd look. "Son, what's his entire name?"

"David Dylan Jones."

Hairy wiggled and scrunched and set his mind to recollecting. "No, lad, this child don't recall. Who'd he come with?"

"Sublette supply outfit. Stayed on." Tal felt all twitchy. "Must have found the life suited him." Tal stretched his arms for relief.

"Left ye with your aunt, did he?" Hairy mused.

Tal saw Hairy's face full of questions and quick decided he'd better do the asking himself.

"Who you working for, Hairy, Hudson Bay?" Which would make sense from the British accent.

"This child labors for himself alone, lad," Hairy retorted.

"Trapping been any good?"

He shook a huge finger at Tal. "There be things in heaven and earth greater than the wily one, lad, sure there be. Greater than putting money in the purse."

"Such as?" Tal felt a little thrill.

Hairy got a bright old gleam in his eye. "Wagh! There be wrongs to right. Honors to win. Colors to strike. Fair maidens to woo. All more worthy of pursuit than filthy luchre."

Hairy eyed Tal peculiarly, like sizing him up. "Yea and verily, lad, this child has had occasion to engage in the odd affair of honor. And acquitted himself valorously."

"What happened?"

Hairy got a cagey look. "Nay, lad, that is for storytelling time. If'n you do something glo-o-orious, the Injuns make a tale of it in the winter, and pass it on among the legends of the people."

The boy's lower lip spoke disappointment.

Hairy shook his head decisively. "No, son, not even for you. Bad medicine."

"Hai-r-r-e-ee!"

"Not even for you. Come winter, I'll tell, or Injun comrades will tell for me. Remember, in the meantime—engaging in affairs of honor is not only ennobling, it's practical. You do something for an Injun, and he'll make a brother of ye. Or she'll give you her favors. Yessir."

Tal got all flushed.

For dinner they gorged on more bear, then laid back and watched the sky go lavender and then gray and then black. Tal had never seen so many stars, thick and clustery.

Hairy was muttering about getting another dream with another griz and being able to find the critter and having better luck in the fair and furious battle. Might not be so easy, he murmured, might not be easy at all.

"But lad, I got to have her. Swee-e-et Spring," he crooned. "This child is misuble to have her. Oh, she's scrumptious, she's delectable." He moaned, he mooned, he nearly swooned.

"Shall I compare ye to a summer's day?"

Tal began to think Hairy had lost too much blood after all.

Hairy rethought his griz strategy. Maybe he should have got a medicine man to show him how to do a bear dance. Maybe should. That bear dance this child did was a slight, actually. But those medicine men didn't give away such knowledge for nothing, and Hairy's peltries, or plews was cached in the Hills, and...

It was getting nippy. Colder than nippy. Hairy built the fire up big, set his saddle by it, laid out some canvas and blankets, and crawled in. He lifted a keg and drank deep.

"'Night, lad," he said. He grinned big as a harvest moon and pushed another keg toward Tal. "Surely do thank you for happening by today." He laid back down. "It was providential. Providential." Another deep swig from the keg.

Tal tasted his—good, sweet, mountain water. He stared at the fire until he started shivering. Then he got in his own bedroll. He was tired, and might have gone straight to sleep, if Hairy hadn't snored like a steamboat whistle.

Tal could ignore it. Gorged, he lay back and closed his eyes, enjoying the cool night. I conquered Old Ephraim, he thought. With one shot. I'm Old One-Shot. And I have a griz skull and jaw bones and claws to start a necklace. Plus a robe to share with the lady of my dreams.

Medicine, magic, fateful dreams, totems, and a brave giant! Enchantments, battles, challenges, and dusky maidens! Wasn't this what he came to the Shining Mountains for? Was this not a subject for heroic verses? Tal was a happy man. Boy. No, man.

Maybe he should write in his notebook now. No, he was embarrassed—Hairy might stir. He'd just think on putting the epic battle of Old Ephraim and Old One-Shot in it. And now he had a title—*Record of My Sojourn in the Shining Mountains: AN AFFAIR OF HONOR.*

Tal squirmed in his blankets. He liked thinking such thoughts—chivalrous thoughts!—but they made him wonder about himself. Wonder if chivalrous thoughts were kid stuff. Maybe such stuff would earn him a name less fine than Old One-Shot. Like Idjit. Or, worse, Boy. It was hard to know.

4

one man in his time plays many parts
— As You Like It, II. vii

He did not dream, though, of chivalry. He dreamt of wandering on foot, hungry and in rags, through a dark forest, pushed onward ever onward by the sense of some will o' the wisp of foreboding.

He woke with the foreboding. Silly, he told himself. Cautiously he opened his eyes to a gray, half-lit sky. Listened—something had woken him up.

Ummm, Hairy's stoking up the fire. Wind's up. Cold as heck.

He sure is building that fire big. Tal snuggled in his blankets, wary of sleep, reluctant to face the cold dawn.

Uh-oh. What's…

Tal sat up, and it took him a moment to understand what he saw.

Hairy was in the bushes trying to get his pants pulled up.

The fire—much too big—was whipping in the wind.

Beyond it a grass fire was whipping in the wind.

Nearby the horses were about to go crazy trying to break their hobbles.

Holy heck.

Tal jumped up. His pants still down, Hairy grabbed some blankets and started beating at the grass fire.

Tal went for the horses, got the halters of all three, started pulling them away, down wind.

When he looked back, Hairy had the grass fire about out.

The main fire, still blowing, was spreading the other way, up the creek.

Tal let go the horses and sprinted toward the fire. He grabbed his water keg and started dousing the logs. Hairy was roaring up the creek with the pot, scooping water as he went, and tripping over his pants.

Tal grabbed Hairy's water keg and emptied it on the logs. Funny smell.

"My whiske-e-ee," Hairy bellowed.

Tal dropped the keg. Too late.

Still bellowing, Hairy waddled into the grass fire. Tal went after him with blankets—that grass fire was going wild. Lucky it was headed upstream.

Hairy turned to face Tal—his beard and hair were smoking and spurting flame at the ends.

Tal threw the blankets over Hairy's head and dragged him back toward camp. To heck with the fire.

Hairy held the whisky keg overhead and poured the dregs on his head. His hair and beard steamed. He licked his lips. He held his pants. He gave way to tears. He cried a Falstaffian cry.

Tal looked toward the horses. They were bucking and jumping, moving away from the acrid smell, downstream. The pack horse had broken its hobbles.

Suddenly a yell. A shout of war. Or of fear. A cacophony of shouts.

Fear washed over Tal. The foreboding of his dream…

Upstream, where the grass fire was still racing away from camp, three Indians came tearing out of the bushes. A man and two boys.

They were shouting, like old women cursing pests. The man shook his fist and they started running—up the hill. And they kept going uphill, full speed ahead.

Lo, Tal thought, we have defeated our enemies.

He didn't even reach for his rifle. He began to laugh.

Hairy, teary-faced, started laughing. They looked at each other.

"They were gonna get our horses," yelled Tal, and laughed harder.

Hairy sobered. "Why do you think I burned them out?" He glared at Tal.

Tal stuck his tongue out at Hairy and made a raspberry.

Hairy looked scandalized. Then sheepish. Then amused. He guffawed. Tal guffawed. They clapped each other on the back, guffawing.

"They woulda got our horses," yelled Hairy. He grabbed Tal by the shoulders and eyeballed him close. "You're sump'n," Hairy gasped between laughs. "My partner's sump'n."

Tal grabbed Hairy by his charred, ashen beard. "They woulda got our horses," yelled Tal, crying as he laughed, and shaking Hairy's lovable giant head. The whiskers were crumbling.

Then it came off—the whole belly-length beard, in Tal's hands.

Tal gaped at Hairy's chin.

Bare, except for glue.

Shakespeare!

"Bard of Avon!" cried Tal, busting with silliness.

"All the world's a stage," intoned Hairy, laughing and crying and slapping his legs and making sheepdog eyes.

Tal stuck the beard on his own boyish face. "One man in his time plays many parts!" he exclaimed.

Hairy lit up like a sun-struck gong. They cackled and clapped each other on the shoulders like giddy fools.

The bear meat would do for Tal's booty—griz would be some for men new to the mountains—so they were off downhill to find the brigade. And Hairy—Shakespeare—regaled Tal with thespian tales as they rode.

After crossing from Olde England, he said, he'd worked the little towns along the Ohio, from Fort

Pitt to Louisville to Cairo, enchanting audiences with Shakespeare, the sweetest songs e'er composed for the English tongue. When his small troupe toured these rustic places, they didn't do entire plays, naturally—those gre-e-a-at cathedrals built of words—but piquant scenes, interspersed with singing and juggling. Hairy's most magnificent role was the great King Lear:

Blow, winds, and crack your cheeks!

Likely his most popular was Falstaff:

Why then the world's mine oyster

or perhaps Caliban:

'Ban, 'Ban, Ca-Caliban,

Has a new master—Get a new man.

But then all changed. The manager fired the lads playing the female parts—that's how the Bard wanted it, you know, teen-age boys as women—and got some actresses.

The troupe switched from the Ohio to the Mississippi, playing Hannibal and St. Louis and Cairo again and Natchez and New Orleans. Hairy could tell some tales about Natchez-under-the-Hill and the French Quarter that would…never you mind. All went well until they began playing the actual river boats. Then the actresses started to mingle with the spectators, and imbibe with them….Well, hoss, Hairy began to tipple more often himself—sometimes, verily, he had trouble remembering his lines. And then the women began to supplement their incomes by dallying with the gentlemen spectators, well, never you mind.

It gave the troupe a bad name, it did, and none of the better theatres would book them anymore. They had to forego the Bard, which the vulgar audience did not appreciate, and sing more songs, songs of the common sort.

And then, ah, hoss, the manager tried to demote Hairy to stage manager. Said Hairy was so drunk he sounded more Kentuck than Shakespearean. A bald-faced lie about the most splendiferous voice in the land, Hairy said resonantly. Fellow just wanted Lear and Falstaff for himself. Hairy couldn't stand still for such impertinence, and broke the fellow's pate.

"But hoss, this child got square, he did." Hairy beamed. "He got square in beards, such as you see, make-up, costumes, and other tools of the actor's sub-tile art and craft. I have a rich stores of such things," Hairy said and chuckled thunderously, "if ever the Injuns should want to lift their spirits by the Bard."

When Hairy wasn't showing off his Shakespeare, he was complaining about Tal dumping his good whisky on the fire. That *aguardiente* cost him five plews the keg to Taos, he said, and they might not see Taos again for months and months.

"You wasn't exactly sharing that awerdenty, now, was ye?" complained Tal mildly. From his dad he learned never to cuss—a matter of style, not moral-ity—but he was willing to try an experimental tipple. Just like his dad.

"That was a fault," admitted Hairy. "Truly, that was a fault."

So down they went, amid story and song. Hairy's riding horse was an odd-looking Indian pony, a gelding. Odd-looking on its own because it was a paint with a patchy, scrofulous coat and a red circle around one blind, gray-mottled eye. Odd-looking under Hairy because the poor creature was no more than thirteen hands high, and sway-backed, while Hairy probably weighed three hundred pounds. Little beast sure was game, though—never slowed or faltered, burdened as it was.

After a while they rode into a thunderstorm, but it gave Hairy no pause.

"This is fine, ain't it lad? "rumbled the giant. "Fine, fine, this child loves the tempest." He raised his voice into the wind.

Blow, winds, and crack your cheeks!
Rage! Blow! You cataracks and hurricanoes, spout
Till you have drench'd our noggins, drown'd our cocks!

When Hairy spoke as Lear, it sounded like organ music. Tal thought maybe it was fine to be here, in foul weather, in the Black Hills of the Shining Mountains. Until he began to shiver and shake. And chatter. While Hairy carried on in grand style, oblivious.

That night they camped in the foothills and, despite incredible heat, went hard the next day. At evening they came onto camp. They put their horses with the others, and sauntered casually into Louie's mess.

"Cap'n Fitzpatrick, he's summat colicky, Jones," Louie volunteered. Louie was old as the hills, a

Frenchy who'd been H. B. C.—Hudson Bay Co., or Here Before Christ, as the men joked.

Louis was looking past Tal to Hairy. Tal had to admit Hairy looked a little strange, his hair singed and broken and his face fishbelly white where the false beard had covered it. He was making sheepdog eyes again, too.

"Louie, this here's my friend, uh, Shakespeare," said Tal.

"What's that smell? "said Louie, eyeing Hairy.

Hairy flushed all the colors of the sunset.

"Our bear meat turned ripe, Louie." The hundred-degree day had overcome their improvised refrigeration. "We made meat, but…"

Louie grinned a grin that seemed almost lecherous. "What you do, sleep with it? Put your bedrolls down wind of me," he said, "and save your explanations for Cap'n Fitzpatrick."

5

here's a young and sweating devil

—Othello, III.iv

Irish Tom Fitzpatrick had his dander up. That kid hadn't reported in and was sitting at Louie's mess like nothing had happened and was with that... damned stray dog.

Things were going badly for Tom Fitzpatrick. His fledgling fur company was saddled with back-breaking debt. He hadn't gotten to St. Louis in time to get his friends to freight supplies to rendezvous—they were committed to Santa Fe. The detour through Santa Fe had wasted over a month, and now he'd missed rendezvous completely. Worst of all, on the way to Santa Fe, Jedediah Smith, Fitz's long-time friend, was murdered by Comanches.

Never a hail-fellow-well-met, Fitz was aggravated this evening by a sour stomach from weeks of jerky and beans and by this kid who went larking off on his own. When Fitz bestirred himself and walked toward

Louie's mess to give a few growls of reprimand, he was bilious.

"Well, Jones, fancy seeing you here," Fitzpatrick called sarcastically across the fire.

"Went hunting, Cap'n," Tal said cheerfully.

The devil take his cheeriness. "Now did you, lad? Is that why the spit is so heavy with roasts?" Naturally, there wasn't any spit. After the usual beans, the boys were having a sociable pipe.

"They killed a griz, Cap'n," mumbled someone. The newcomer, the stray called Shakespeare, was smiling like a dog wanting to be patted. Something had recently torn his ear off, he was pretty scratched, and his hair looked burnt. Some griz-slayer.

"Did *they*, now?" Cap'n cast a caustic eye on Shakespeare. "So where's the meat?"

"Sp'iled on the way in, Cap'n." Shakespeare's voice was lachrymose.

Godawmighty. Holy Mother. "Jones, I'll see at you my fire at dark. Your friend, too."

Fitzpatrick walked away, nodding Louis along with him.

"You went off without leave," Fitz snapped across the fire at Tal. "Why?"

"Get fresh meat for the men, sir." Kid couldn't look Fitz in the face. Fitz kept the two standing. Louis was squatted next to Fitz.

"Against orders. And no meat."

"Yessir." Eyes still cast down.

"I used up time, men, and horses trying to find you."

"Yessir."

"Aught to say for yourself?"

"Nossir."

"Jones, maybe I shouldn't have brought a youngster like you. You can't take discipline."

Tal's eyes were anchored to his feet. He shifted his weight back and forth.

"You endangered the searchers."

Tal didn't respond.

"Jones, I'm talking to you. Do you understand what you did?"

"Endangered the searchers, sir."

Fitzpatrick eyed him hard. Kid did look like he understood. "Instead I'm fining you the week's pay." Which was lenient.

"Yessir."

"And, kid, galavanting around Injun country lonesome is the best way to get yourself dead."

"Yessir."

"Galavanting with a flaming silk hanky flying from your wiping stick, especially," added Fitz. He gave Louie an exasperated look. The Frenchie smothered a grin.

Tal had nothing to say.

"Tal done good," Shakespeare protested. "He…"

Fitz waved him quiet. The captain gazed into the fire a moment—he wasn't the sort to twist his hands, or pull at his ears—then looked thoughtfully at Tal. He motioned the two of them to sit on a log.

Fitzpatrick looked at Tal Jones, just a boy, really, an orphan boy. Fitz made himself talk at the stray-dog giant.

"What's your proper name, Shakespeare?"

"Ronald Smythe, rhymes with scythe," murmured the giant like a big wind.

Fitz looked at Louie, and the old Frenchie shrugged.

"Wanting to come along?" Fitz asked.

Hairy looked at Tal, almost winked, and said, "Certainly."

Fitz considered. "I don't know you, Smythe, and neither does Louie." Tal felt like the cap'n was going to add, "And I don't like you," but he didn't.

"When we meet up with my partners, maybe someone will vouch for you. Meanwhile you can ride along. But you won't be on payroll." The captain let it sit a moment. "That's all."

Tal and Hairy started away.

"Oh, and Smythe," Fitzpatrick added. Hairy stopped and turned back. "You'd best earn your grub in work. Which in your case will be plenty."

"Yessir."

6

Madness is the glory of this life

—Timon of Athens, I.ii

The next morning, amid heehawing mules and cursing teamsters, Fitzpatrick's brigade started up the North Platte toward the Sweetwater River and the Shining Mountains, bolstered by the addition of Tal and Shakespeare, who were flying the blazon of the House of Jones.

It meant a couple of weeks of daylight-to-dusk swaying on top of Rosie, which Tal didn't like. "Lad," Hairy said cheerily, "this child's gonna chat up the ladies."

That's what he did—walked that scrofulous pony alongside the travois that two squaws were escorting and played the gay rogue. He looked good in the role, laughing merrily, making eyes, and generally carrying on.

Both squaws seemed too well used to attract that sort of attention, Tal thought—well used by Louie, probably, who was keeping a proprietary eye on them. Hairy looked a little different himself, dwarfing his pint-sized, half-blind horse, his ear scratched down to a stub, his hair burned and scraggly, like a Lear who'd got too close to the lightning. But you'd never know he wasn't a dashing Launcelot, the way he was carrying on.

After a while Hairy rode back and talked with Louie for a while, and Louie seemed to converse amiably enough. When Hairy came back, he had a mischievous smile, the sort that was beginning to seem worrisome. "Lad, tonight this child will initiate you into one of the mysteries of the muse."

He spoke of the mysteries of the muse three or four times. When Tal asked what the devil he meant, Hairy fingered some of his raggedy hair and said, "We'll repair my manhood."

"Grease her good, lad, that's the trick."

Hairy was stretched out full length, his head propped on his saddle, and Tal was greasing the top of his balding head. Hairy watched in two small hand-held mirrors. Satisfied, he handed Tal the straight razor.

The men ten yards away at their coffee were affecting not to notice, but they were smirking.

Tal was dubious. The broken and burned hair did look pretty wretched. But shave the whole head? It came off easily enough, though not what Tal would have called close.

"Not there, lad, not that spot. Save that. I'll show ye." The spot was behind and above one ear, the thickest hair Hairy had left.

Before long Tal was finished. Not a bad job, altogether. Except for that one patch, which looked like an armpit. Tal tugged at it.

"No, lad," resonated Hairy. He sat up off the saddle and felt of the patch and looked at it with his two mirrors. "Take a while to grow out, but when it does, this child will braid it and have a scalplock.

"Know why a scalplock is your manhood, lad?"

Tal knew he didn't need to answer.

"On account of it gives the coon that scalps ye something to grip on to." Hairy was smiling his ogre smile. "He slips his finger under the braid and just p-p-pops her off." He was practically licking his lips.

Hairy started rummaging in a parfleche carrying case. "Now a *jefe grande* like this child don't like to go around without plenty of hair to get hold of. Don't want anyone to think he's skittish about losing his scalp. Enough scalplock to braid by winter. Meantime…"

He held it up proudly. At first Tal thought it was a prime fur, so thick and fine and chestnut brown it was. Then he saw the luxuriant curls. A wig, almost shoulder length. Hairy pulled it onto his head and tugged till it looked just right in the mirror. Hairy intoned,

I am of Percy's mind, the Hotspur of the West, he that kills me some six or seven dozen of Scots at a breakfast, washes his hands, and says to his wife, 'Fie upon this quiet life!'

Hairy modelled it for Tal, turning his big head this way and that. Tal thought it handsome, adding a touch of gallant to Hairy's natural fierce.

"And will ye dance with us, Ronald?" one of the boys called in an Irish lilt. They were ten steps away, lounging around a low cook fire.

Another one, his elbow against a wagon, mimicked in Pennsylvania Dutch, "Aye, and a kisch for two bitsch, mine beauty."

Hairy sized him up for a moment, there off to the left of the others, then reached leisurely behind his belt and whipped his arm toward the mimicker.

The knife whacked into the wagon snug against the man's elbow, its handle quivering.

"Ah, ye can keep the knife, lad," rumbled Hairy. "It throws a mite low." He smiled his ogre smile, huge and mean.

"You sumbitch," the man snarled.

"Shut up, pantywaist." The words came from the Irish lilter. Tal couldn't figure it.

"Vas?" growled Pennsylvania Dutch.

Hairy was just grinning like a polecat.

"You dress like Little Lord Fauntleroy, and your sis does too," sang Irish. Except that his mouth didn't move, and he looked bewildered. Pennsylvania Dutch moved toward him, Hairy's knife held low.

Hairy picked up the saddle and slipped off. Tal followed close behind.

Tal could hear the other men interfering, stopping the fight. "That's a trick of Shakespeare's," someone hollered. "He didn't insult ye, Dutch."

Others were calling out words like "crazy" and "half-wit."

"How'd you do it, Hairy?"

"A bit of the actor's craft, lad." He sang this sentence in an uncanny imitation of the Irish lilter—not just the accent, but voice itself. "Ve showed zem, didn't ve?" This was Dutch, right down to the rasp. "Mimicry plus ventriloquism." Tal noticed his mouth didn't move at all. Incredible.

Hairy took Tal's arm and kept him walking, on the quick.

"Wagh!" said Tal. That was the kind of crazy Tal liked.

Next morning Hairy brought it up to Tal. He'd been chatting up the two squaws for about an hour when he suddenly cantered back to Tal, his chestnut locks bouncing and a big smile on his face.

"The real statuesque one," said Hairy, pointing. "Name is Iron Kettle."

Bound to be trouble, thought Tal. "The bony one?" The older, homelier squaw who was always talking so fast with tongue and hands at once. "She belongs to Louie."

"Naw, she don't. I found out about her. She was sharing blankets with a coon back to Taos, been with him since last summer, and took a notion. Likely he lodgepoled her, or beat her when he was drunk, or some such." Hairy's British accent seemed to come and go more now.

"Anyhow, she left him and rode this way with Louie on account of he said the brigade might go on to the Stinking Water. Her people will be there in the fall. Maybe she wants her buck back. Or just wants home cooking."

Tal regarded her. She looked old as river rock, and too worn for anyone to want, in his opinion.

"So what's the object?"

"Hoss, this child ain't whole-hog comfortable in this place."

"And?"

"Her folks would think mighty well of the beavers what brought her home. Mighty well. Several horses well."

It dawned on Tal. "You mean escort her?" He pondered it. It sounded appealing, but dangerous.

"Where's the Stinking Water?"

"Well, hoss, ain't so far. Over that divide to the north, and down the Big Horn."

The country to the north was flat sagebrush plain, dry, hot, and hellish in August. Beyond it high peaks rose, some with eternal snow.

"How many sleeps?" Tal meant to be careful where he stepped.

"Not so many, lad. She'll know. Iron Kettle will know. Not so many."

Tal made a skeptical face. On second thought, it would be nuts to strike out alone. As Hairy was nuts, generally.

Besides…

"Naw, Hairy, I can't." He shook his head decisively. "I *got* to go to rendezvous. I got to find out…"

Shouts. Guns firing.

Somewhere ahead.

Tal pulled Rosie out and spotted Cap'n Fitz at the head of the column. Cap'n was holding up an arm, but taking no action.

Tal looked to his priming. He waited—and waiting hurt.

In two or three minutes men came sliding on horseback down the sand hills toward the brigade. They were whooping and shooting in the air. White men. Friends.

Quickly the word came back. Frapp's brigade was just ahead. Rendezvous had come to them.

7

bewitched with the rogue's company

—Henry IV, Part 1, II. ii

The partners, Fitzpatrick and Frapp, sat long and traded news. Fitz told why he had to go to Santa Fe and so was late. Frapp told about the difficult spring trapping season, about how he and Gabe and Milton and Gervais had struggled, about everyone waiting for Fitz to show up at rendezvous, and about hiring a medicine man to tell the partners where Fitz was.

Tom Fitzpatrick, Henry Fraeb (pronounced Frapp), Gabe Bridger, Milton Sublette, and Jean Gervais were the partners of Rocky Mountain Fur Company, which had bought out 'Diah Smith's outfit.

Before long it was all over camp how Fitz was mad at the way his partners had squandered company money to find Fitzpatrick.

"You hired a what?" Fitz spat.

"A Crow man great of medicine," answered Frapp. Frapp was a German, and sometimes his English was twisted. "When you ware late, ve vas werry vorried. 'Fraid maybe you ware gone under."

"How many company horses did you pay for this nonsense?" Fitz himself was an unbeliever. It was his opinion and observation that those who subscribed to the Christian superstition slipped easily into Indian superstition.

"Yah, vell, this fellow he conjure much."

All the mountain men knew how it worked. The old fellow would screech and dance and mesmerize himself with the beat of the drum until he passed out—that might take days—and then call his fevered dreams a vision. Some of the old hands told the new-comers this story with superior glances. It had worked, hadn't it? Fitz's lot had been on the wrong road.

While the partners made their plans, their men ate, smoked, and gossiped. Tal was excited by these fellows, these authentic men of the Shining Mountains in a fire-hardened brigade of several dozen, complete with Indian wives and children. Some of them looked half Indian themselves, dressed in breechcloths and leggings, shod in mocassins, their hair down past their shoulders. A tough lot, Tal thought, seasoned men of sanguine disposition, worthy to be among:

Scots, what hae wi' Wallace bled,
Scots, wham Bruce has aften led,
Welcome to your gory bed,
Or to victorie.

Tal looked forward to hearing these men tell of titanic battles with Indians, of fierce struggles against the elements, of miracles and miseries, of comrades lost and saved. He longed to be one of these comrades himself, and felt pride in anticipation.

Over pemmican and coffee Louie announced the partners' plan. There would be no rendezvous this year—it was too late. Frapp would turn back to the mountains with the supplies Cap'n Fitzpatrick had brought and distribute them as other brigades were encountered. Fitz would head to St. Louis now with last year's peltries, sell them, and return to supply next year's rendezvous.

Some of Fitzpatrick's men would be hired for the mountains—some would go back—those wanting the mountains could talk to the clerk. "Meanwhile, for right now," said Louie with a slow grin, "Cap'n Fitzpatrick is tapping a keg. Bring your cups."

And the evening air filled with hurrahs.

"You'll have to check with the cap'n," said the clerk. "He listed ye bound back to the States."

So Tal said he'd stroll through the cool night air and find Fitzpatrick. Hairy allowed that he'd get a cupful and keep Tal company. "Wagh, lad," he said, "I'll not sign on, though. This child means to stay a free trapper."

"How's that, Hairy?"

"Well, if'n ye sign on, they fit ye out with traps and other possibles and put ye on wages. That's good, that's real good," Hairy said.

Tal prompted him. "What's bad about it?"

"It's a boon to ride in a troop, 'cause there be safety in numbers in Injun country. And ye learn the country that way, some," Hairy allowed.

"Come on, Hairy."

"Wagh! Lad, this child likes being his own man. A free trapper rides with the troop when he likes, rides as he will when he doesn't. Sells his plews where he wants, and when. Traps when he pleases, dallies when he don't. There be more things in the world, lad, than catching big, hairy water rats." Hairy gave his fierce grin.

Tal figured he'd sign on anyway. "It's good for newcomers," Hairy agreed. "I'll trail along with ye, unofficial, for the nonce."

"Nay," said Fitzpatrick. "It's the States and no argument." Even over the boisterousness of drinking men, the captain's soft voice sounded authoritative.

Tal took a swig of whisky for show and looked across the fire at the two partners. "Captain," said Tal in his firmest voice, "I have to go to rendezvous. That's what I signed on for."

"There'll be no rendezvous this year."

"To the mountains, then."

"Why, Jones?"

Tal scuffed his feet. Hairy was hanging way back, sipping his whisky and watching. Frapp was watching too, curiously.

"Jones, I signed you on because Sublette said you were a hunter, young as you are. And it's true, you got the gift. You can feed us going home." Fitzpatrick kept shifting his eyes from Tal to Hairy, waiting for something.

"I got to go on, Cap'n."

Fitzpatrick took a moment to light a pipe. "Better speak up, lad."

"My dad ran off to the mountains, sir."

"I heard."

"I want to find him, sir."

"David Dylan Jones, his name is. I checked it out. Came out with Sublette two years ago. The company doesn't know where he is now, son. Probably went straight back. Like you."

"No, sir, he didn't come back," Tal said, making an effort to sound sure.

"What's zis man look like?" put in Frapp.

Tal pictured his father the preacher, a willowy sort of man with buck teeth and a wonderful childish smile. He put words to the picture gingerly, trying to sound factual.

Fitz and Frapp nodded at each other.

"Man with a way with a story," Frapp said.

Tal nodded, his throat lumping. Yes, Dad's a miracle with a story.

"Likeable fellow, none so practical," Frapp muttered to Fitzpatrick. "I remember him. Maybe he was the one with 'Diah who went…No, is probably wrong man."

"He's not with the company now," said Fitzpatrick. "I checked. Likely he's gone under or gone home," said the captain bluntly. "And the Rocky Mountains are too big a haystack to rummage through, lad."

Tal wasn't hearing Fitzpatrick, he was hearing Dad, Dad sounding out the words of a hymn, looking shy and boyishly simple at the pulpit raising hosannas unto the Lord.

"I got to go, Cap'n."

"And I can't hire you on, son," Fitzpatrick said regretfully. "You're a good hand for a lad, but you're still a lad. Can't do it."

"Shakespeare will see me through," Tal said bravely.

"I will that, Tal Jones," Hairy rumbled from behind.

"That doesn't help, son," said Fitzpatrick. "Makes it worse." He hesitated. "Found out some about your friend this evening."

"I remember zis fellow," said Frapp, eyeing Hairy shrewdly. "Shakespeare. Come with Provo. Used to been actor." Frapp shook his head, cocked an eye at Hairy, shook his head emphatically.

"Better speak out," said Fitz.

"I hear he vorks alone on account of his partners ditched him. Acts too crazy. Ditched him for true. And...No damn good."

Tal didn't stop it. He felt unfaithful—unfaithful to Hairy, or to Dad. "Be particular," said Fitzpatrick.

Hairy was glaring theatrically at Frapp.

Frapp made a little face. "He cleaned his partners out. Won it all at three-card monte. Then like fool shows them trick so they can cheat Injuns too. Is charlatan."

Hairy turned conspicuously to stare off into space, his missing ear facing everyone. Tal could have hit him.

"That so, Hairy?" Tal rasped.

"Legerdemain, lad. Prestidigitation. One of the actor's stocks in trade."

"If you were going to stay in the mountains, Jones," Fitzpatrick added gently, "you couldn't choose..."

"He's my partner," Tal interrupted. It sounded like a dare.

All three heads jerked toward Tal. Silence.

"Jones," said Fitz gently, "you're a beginner."

"He's my *partner,*" Tal said, his words like a wall.

"Son," began Fitz...

Tal lifted a hand at the cap'n. The hand was trembling.

"He's my friend."

Tal was tongue-tied. He felt words would come out sobs. "Know what he did up in the Hills?" Tal blurted. "A griz attacked him and he killed it with his tomahawk." Now he was babbling. "See those scratches? Those are from the griz. Shakespeare stood up to it with just his 'hawk. And killed the sumbuck. I saw it."

It was a child's voice, pleading. He had to make them understand.

"When some Injuns were about to steal our horses, he burned them out and made them hightail it."

Fitz and Frapp eyed each other.

"He's my friend. My partner." Said defiantly.

Fitz stood up. "I can't do it, son," said Fitz softly. "I'm sorry."

Dismissed, Tal and Hairy walked slowly into the dark. Tal had never felt such a roil of…of everything, like all the songs he'd ever known jumbled and clashing. He blinked, and tears ran down his cheeks.

Hairy didn't talk. Just looked down, as if moping. Walked right into a giant sagebrush. Fell down.

Tal smiled. He laughed a little, a teary laugh. He could hear Hairy's big rumbling chuckle, too. Tal stuck a hand down. Hairy took it and pulled Tal down and rolled him over and held his shoulders to the ground, like when Jacob wrestled the angel. Tal could see Hairy's teeth and eyes gleaming in the dark, inches away.

"Thanks, partner," hissed Hairy.

"Anything for a partner, partner," said Tal, faking wryness. He pushed. "Lemme up."

Hairy jumped up and pulled Tal to his feet.

"I got an idea, partner," Hairy whispered hugely.

"An idea?"

8

O brave new world

—The Tempest, V.i

The next morning, in the pre-dawn light, openly and defiantly, Tal and Hairy left the brigade and rode off for the forks of the Stinking Water, the Crow squaw Iron Kettle behind them.

"Besides, lad, it's adventure," Hairy cajoled. "It's a chivalrous deed, it's the stuff of heroic couplets."

"What does trapping big, smelly water rats get you, anyway?" quipped Tal.

Tal had the orange and azure handkerchief flying from his wiping stick. Thus the blazon of the House of Jones headed into the land of the Absarokas, the people of the mountain raven.

"Getting killed will be something new," Tal added.

Tal wished Hairy and Iron Kettle wouldn't be so noisy about it. Their, uh, mating, that is. He didn't like that word for it, but he liked the other words less.

Love it certainly wasn't. Love was…not all this braying, whickering, roaring, moaning…

Love meant more like what Tal had felt with Guadalupe in Santa Fe. Guadalupe. He'd watched her all evening. While her companion, perhaps her chaperone, danced with hidalgo and campesino and buckskinned trapper alike, arms bare, bodice daring, and skirts flouncing—while the older woman carried on thus wantonly, Guadalupe stood decorously against the wall and observed. She was slender, pale, and virginally beautiful in a white dress accented by colored silk handkerchiefs in her hair. When suitors came to ask her to dance, and then left with stiff, courteous smiles, Tal could see she was as tall as most of them. Though men pinched the bottom of her flirting, smiling, teasing companion, by common consent they treated the tall, demure Guadalupe with chivalry.

In the shank of the evening, a boozy shank, Tal turned and saw an hidalgo talking loudly and rudely to Guadalupe. She was casting her eyes about nervously, but the other woman was busy with a flirtation. Tal gulped, squared his shoulders, crossed the room, and wordlessly offered Guadalupe his arm. Without a backward glance she took it and steered Tal toward the musicians. She spoke a few soft words, and in a moment the music changed to a minuet. Guadalupe led Tal to the center of the floor, held his hand high, and began a measured, stately dance. Most of the others backed away to watch. Not knowing the dance, Tal took an occasional step with her, but mostly held her hand aloft while she danced to him. It made him feel honored.

After the dance the chaperone took them both by the arm and hustled them onto the patio. "What a beautiful, young Americano," she said to Guadalupe, looking into Tal's eyes playfully, "beautifully innocent." She squeezed his arm. "I thank you on behalf of my sister, who has little English. That was gallant." She made a little curtsy, as though taking leave.

"Perhaps the *elegante* Americano escorts us home," Guadalupe said haltingly.

"Of course," murmured Tal.

So the sister performed the introductions—they were Guadalupe and Carlotta Echeverria—and they strolled through the cool summer evening.

Taking leave at the door of their house, the sort of house common frontiersmen were not permitted to enter, Guadalupe reached behind her head, took off the orange and azure handkerchief in her rolled hair, and slipped the comb out. She shook her gleaming black hair onto her shoulders, charmingly disarrayed. Then she kissed the handkerchief and held it against Tal's cheek. When he covered her hand with his, she slipped hers away, leaving the handkerchief.

Murmuring *"Buenas noches,"* she slipped inside.

Tal rubbed his cheek with the handkerchief, then held it away to see it. A lady's colors. A banner to carry. Tal didn't know what to do. He felt an impulse to serenade beneath her window. But he hadn't the nerve. Wandering back toward camp, he hummed a minor-key English folk song that had been a favorite of his father's:

Greensleeves was all my love,
And Greensleeves was my delight.
Greensleeves was my heart of gold,
And who but the lady Greensleeves?

After that evening with Guadalupe, he didn't even know why Hairy would want these episodes of galumphing carnality with Iron Kettle. He himself had made a decision: He would forego casual sex. True, Tal had sexual urges, sexual aches. And in this world of Indians, sex was available enough. But he would wait for romance.

It was a decision that was unusual, that might make his fellows think him strange. He liked that.

One morning over coffee Hairy got to explaining. Iron Kettle was a woman and expected to be used as a woman—by her trapper mate, her buck, by Louie, by Hairy, by whatever man she was with. Naturally. (By Tal as well, Hairy hinted, but Tal affected not to understand.) Crows were like that. Most Injuns were like that. When in Rome, Hairy intoned, do as the Romans do. Which, to Tal, was all right for Hairy.

And it wasn't that he didn't like Iron Kettle. She was cheerful. She wouldn't let either of the men gather wood or get water or cook, or do anything in camp but relax. She had a wicked sense of humor, and told the dirtiest jokes Tal had ever heard. She delighted in getting Hairy's wig and aping his walk and his talk and all about him. She was willing in the blankets, clearly.

Tal approved of her. But what was romantic about her? What was inspiring, uplifting, ennobling? Really, this avid humping did make Tal wrinkle his nose.

They'd struck north from the Sweetwater across dry, barren hills and come straight to where the Popo Agie flowed into Wind River, as Iron Kettle said they would. Down the Wind and through its narrow, Whitewater canyon into greener country on the north side of the mountains. They spent several days hunting antelope and drying meat and soaking in the huge hot springs there (and for some reason the river changed its name to the Big Horn). That was where the two of them started acting like honeymooners. On along the west side of this big basin they'd travel, Iron Kettle said. The people would be at the forks of the Stinking Water River, sooner or later. This was the land of the Absarokas, Crow country—filled with friends, with plenty of game, good water, warm days and cool nights—why rush? They rode up Owl Creek and over a low divide to a nameless creek and another to another no-name creek and pushed higher into the mountains to avoid the heat. Near the timber the days were cool, the nights nippy, hinting of winter. Tal saw a coyote already getting prime, and Hairy said it would be a hard winter.

In a fine, narrow valley on the Greybull River they stopped to take a few elk. Iron Kettle built six-foot-high racks and dried long strips over a low, low fire. She stretched and tanned Tal's bear robe, and a couple of elk robes as well, to give him warmth for the winter. While Tal lay about reading his favorite passages in *Scottish Chiefs,* Hairy and Iron Kettle lay about in the little lean-to, enjoying each other. Even Tal began to smile about it. This was an idyllic time, a time such as Sir William Wallace had, in his mountain aerie, before his countrymen called him forth to bloody deeds.

In the evenings Iron Kettle told stories about bloody deeds, the sallies of the Absaroka people (whom the white men call the Crows) against their ancient enemies the Siksikas, or Blackfeet. She would not tell medicine stories, but she told of fights, horses stolen, scalps taken.

She thrilled in a way unbecoming to a lady, thought Tal, in talking of blood running down her arm from a fresh scalp—but then Iron Kettle was no lady. And Hairy said Injun women were more bloodthirsty than the men. They were a barbaric people, thought Tal, but not so different from the Scot clans fighting for their hereditary lands against the hated Englanders. Barbarism touched with magnificence.

"One of our warriors is a Long Knife," Iron Kettle put forward one evening. She handed Hairy the social pipe and the plug.

"And one a woman," added Hairy.

Iron Kettle gave him a strange look.

"A black-skinned Long Knife," she went on to Tal. She adjusted the pot on the fire. "Antelope."

"Jim Beckwourth," Hairy said. He lit his pipe with some char cloth. "Lives with the Crows. I knowed him since '25." He blew smoke to the four directions, the earth, and the sky, and handed Tal the pipe.

"He fights like man of great medicine," Iron Kettle said with a lusty smile, "and comes home painted black." Tal drew deep on the pipe. Painted black meant being victorious, he'd heard. Iron Kettle's broken English was pretty good.

"He ruts like one too," Hairy said. "If you think this child likes the blankets…How he and that Pine Leaf have any time for scalping I don't know."

"Hairy!" Iron Kettle said sharply. "Pine Leaf will not marry until she has taken a hundred Blackfoot scalps. She sleeps in no man's blankets."

She looked at Tal, debating, but there was no way Tal was going to let Iron Kettle get by without telling the story of Pine Leaf now. A woman warrior—no one had heard of such a thing! On the way to a hundred scalps of the fightingest Indians on the Plains. This was martial music.

Pine Leaf had a twin brother, a teen-ager, Iron Kettle told it, who was killed by the Blackfeet. She loved this brother as a sister would, and maybe even more—her medicine, she said, was to avenge his death. She began to practice with the bow and the spear with the young boys. Soon she had a strong arm, and was more accurate than any of them. When the men would not let her go with the war parties, even to hold the horses, she left camp alone and came back with Siksika ponies. This would have been the most daring deed that any boy-warrior had ever done, to steal horses for the first time alone. For a woman truly extraordinary. Some of the people began to believe that her medicine might be for war.

Tal reloaded the pipe and lit it, keeping his eyes averted from Iron Kettle, so as not to look too eager.

The leading warriors, though, said that she could not go on the warpath. How could a woman share the warpath secret? Iron Kettle, like the other women, wasn't quite sure what this warpath secret was, but it was of high importance, essential to the success of the party, and never under any circumstances to be revealed or even referred to after it was told.

"This child," Hairy put in, "thinks they tells how they've been diddling each other's women. They 'fesses up before battle."

Iron Kettle gave him a disgusted look.

So, Iron Kettle went on, with a smirk of satisfaction, she went out alone. (Tal was thinking how he'd write this part down: The warrior-woman, denied her destiny by the conventions of the tribe, ventured forth on faith alone, encountered the enemy by stealth at night...) She stole more ponies—and this time came back with the scalp of the pony guard.

The counselors of the tribe scarcely knew what to do about such a woman, and such deeds. How could they praise a woman who behaved as a man? How could they condemn anyone who took Blackfoot scalps? "Old Jim helped them see the light," Hairy said, chuckling.

"It's true," Iron Kettle went on. Tal stuck the pipe toward her and she looked at him like he was nuts before he remembered, and handed the pipe to Hairy. "It was then that Antelope came back to the people. He had been stolen as a child but now returned to his parents as a man."

"Leastwise that was the story he give out," said Hairy. "Handy, it was."

Iron Kettle glared at Hairy.

"I think Antelope had big eyes for Pine Leaf right away," she mused. "And he was taken with the idea that a woman could be a warrior. Maybe he wanted to be her teacher. From the beginning she was more a comrade. They dared each other, spurred each other to greater deeds. In winter I will tell you some— Antelope himself will probably tell you some. They avenged the deaths of many Absarokas on the heads of the Blackfeet."

Since Pine Leaf refused him, Iron Kettle explained, Antelope took other wives, first one, then a second, then a third. Hairy was nodding happily.

Inevitably, Pine Leaf was accepted on the warpath, admitted even to the warpath secret. She became not merely accepted but admired, then followed, at last celebrated. Warriors old and young, of no coups and many coups, took the warpath under her leadership because her bloodlust was insatiable, her courage great, her judgment keen, her medicine strong.

"Antelope Jim is our most powerful warrior," finished Iron Kettle, "except that maybe Pine Leaf is."

She gave Hairy a wicked smile and crawled into the lean-to. Tal could hear her snuggling into the blankets. Hairy winked broadly and followed her in. Tal went to the water and spread his blankets on the warm, sunned sand. He fell asleep to the sound of elk bugling, which at least covered Hairy's bugling.

He awoke the next morning to find their horses gone.

9

O most pernicious woman!

—Hamlet, I.v

It was a clean sweep—Hairy's broken-down pair, Iron Kettle's riding horse and pack horse, and Rosie.

"Why, you…," Hairy began. "How could you be sleeping out there and not hear anything?"

"Big stupid," put in Iron Kettle. "Between the bugling of the bull elk and the bugling of the bull Hairy, how could anybody hear?"

Tal was looking around for tracks. "What kind of moccasin is this?" he said in a deliberately businesslike way, pointing.

Hairy and Iron Kettle came and bent over it.

"Crow," said Hairy. *"Crow?"*

"Yah," said Iron Kettle. "Is my moccasin." She whomped Hairy on the back, only half-playfully.

"How we gonna catch them on foot?" muttered Hairy.

Tal was checking out other prints in the dust where the horses had been picketed. "I think this one's different," he called. He spotted several more like it, small fragments and large, twisting in all directions.

Iron Kettle stooped. Then she gave a little wobbling, dying cry, a cry that sounded like fear itself. "Blackfoot. So far into our country." Iron Kettle was looking at Hairy. "Black-foot raiders. And me with a big stupid and a boy."

Hairy was strapping on his belt, with knife and tomahawk. "Let's go, lad, time's a-wasting."

"No!" cried Iron Kettle. "They are Blackfoot! They'll kill us!" She clung to Hairy. Hairy gave a Tal a hard look, and Tal got his gun and his spyglass.

"If they were going to kill us, woman, they'd have done it last night." He shook Iron Kettle off. "Probably just boys."

"Is only one sleep to Stinking Water," wailed Iron Kettle. "We walk there, my people help us."

Hairy looked at her indulgently. "We ain't going in empty-handed, lass." He turned to Tal. "Let's move."

It was an obvious trail of a dozen horses, down the Grey-bull toward the Big Horn. Tal wondered if they were being begged to follow it. No, Hairy said, the boys just didn't care because they thought they couldn't be caught. Hairy meant to surprise them.

Tal thought he might do it. Hairy moved at a surprisingly fast lope for a big man, a lope that would overtake a horse that wasn't being pushed. After two hours without a let-up, Tal was struggling to keep up, and didn't think any critters on earth could stay ahead.

At noon the trail turned sort of back on itself, up a little creek that came out of the mountains. They drank quickly and moved on. Hairy was pushing now, grimly, and Tal was dragging.

By late afternoon they knew where they were headed. The trail went up the creek and took a turn back toward camp, straight over a divide. Hairy led them higher, so they could look into camp without being seen on the back trail. Maybe they slowed down because of the steepness, or because they were afraid of what they'd find at camp.

From their perch they could glass the entire valley of the Greybull, including the lean-to by the mouth of the creek. Still breathing hard, Tal recognized Rosie and the others staked beyond camp. He couldn't see any people.

Hairy motioned down with his head and started contouring agilely around the side of the hill. Evidently he meant to stay high, where they could see.

But there was nothing to see. Now the lean-to was just a hundred yards away. No one was visible. The swoosh of the creek and the river kept them from hearing much. Suddenly a woman's cry carried to them. Hairy sat and pondered. The cry came two or three times more.

"We gotta get her," he said. "I think there's only four or five of them, probably boys. Must be using her hard. Raping bastards. Good thing they're so careless."

He threw back his chestnut curls suddenly and rose to a squat. "Still, may be a guard. Best be cautious."

He pulled at his nose, watching the lean-to. It was on the sand in a big bend, opposite a cutbank. Both the ropes that held up the front end of the lean-to stretched across the creek to a tree on the cutbank.

"I'm gonna sneak over and cut those ropes," he said, pointing. "That'll bring the front down and give them trouble coming out. May subdue them pretty good. You get cover over there. If they come out fighting, shoot their lights out."

Tal nodded. He's never shot a person before. Except Hairy.

"Keep your eyes open for a guard." Hairy eased off.

Tal primed his pistol, checked the priming on his rifle, and moved downhill in the other direction. He didn't like any of it.

It took Hairy a long time to circle and come out on the cutbank. Finally Tal saw him steal out of the trees. Immediately he reached out and slashed one rope, bounded over and slashed the other one.

The lean-to collapsed. Iron Kettle screamed.

Hairy stepped to the edge of the cutbank and roared. Roared like a griz, shook his fists, and jumped up and down.

The bank collapsed. Hairy crashed into the water on his back.

Iron Kettle was still screaming. And battle cries were coming from somewhere.

Three Indians, probably teen-agers, ran out of the trees and jumped down the cutbank and grabbed Hairy. Hairy was still on his back, maybe stunned. They held him down in the shallow water.

Tal dropped to his knees and lifted his rifle.

An arm circled his throat. A knife point pricked the underside of his chin. A woman's voice snapped, "Put it down."

Tal laid his rifle down. A foot went onto it. A hand undid his belt, let belt and knife and pistol drop to the ground.

"Watch!" the woman's voice commanded in Tal's ear.

Iron Kettle crawled out from under the lean-to. She was bent over, holding her belly. She pointed at Hairy and the boys, yelling something in Crow. Then the English words, "Scalp him, scalp the bastard."

Heck, she was laughing, uncontrollably.

The arm around his neck dropped away. The knife backed off.

One of the boys made a sweeping motion with his knife, held up Hairy's luxuriant brown wig, and yelled, "Hi-yi-yi-yi!" The boys were whooping and slapping their thighs.

Hairy's scalplock hung pitifully beside his ear, and his naked scalp gleamed in the sunlight.

A hand grasped for Tal's right hand. He faced a woman, young, handsome, teeth gleaming in a big smile, eyes alight.

"Hello," she said. "I am Pine Leaf, warrior woman of the Absaroka people." Stupidly, Tal shook her hand.

Now Hairy was sitting up in the water, feeling of his sticky, shaven head, and staring at the face of Iron Kettle, who was cackling.

Pine Leaf modelled Hairy's wig, and said she had no intention of giving it back. "If you keep a guard so poor," said Pine Leaf, "you deserve."

She picked up a rib and started gnawing, enjoying herself hugely. *"Deserve?"* She looked at Iron Kettle. Pine Leaf felt uncertain about the English she'd been picking up from Antelope Jim. Iron Kettle nodded. "Deserve.

"Sure, if'n I have such horses," Pine Leaf went on, "I beg the Siksikas to steal them."

The four boys were gorging themselves, and making eyes about the wonderful joke. They still had the Blackfoot moccasins on their feet. "I take what I like from the Siksikas, moccasins included," said Pine Leaf casually.

She was a tall, strapping woman with broad, blunt features. A scar made a vertical line from one cheek to the corner of her mouth—it made a pucker when she talked. Some men would have thought her plain, mannish. Tal thought hers a face of barbaric magnificence.

She flipped the wig back to Hairy. "What's a scalp without blood?" she said. She tried to rub the glue off her hands.

The fire was popping with the fat dripping from a spit full of deer ribs. The evening light in the valley of the Greybull River looked lavender, and long shadows lay on the grass. Does and fawns grazed on the benches above the river. Tal would have been stupendously happy except for being embarrassed.

Pine Leaf was by turns vivacious, prickly, mischievous, proud, sympathetic. She looked great in the wig, and her smile was wondrous. Tal thought her scar pucker was very dear. The whole thing had been her idea.

She had taken these kids (they looked fourteen or fifteen, just boys beside Tal's sixteen) to look for some Sioux to steal horses from, on the headwaters of Powder River. Boys need to learn. But for some reason the Sioux were not hunting buffalo there this year, and the North Platte was too far, so they were coming home disappointed when they found tracks headed up the Greybull. Didn't take long to spot the lean-to and the Long Knives. They were delighted to see Iron Kettle.

But what miserable—is *miserable* the word?—camp-making. No guard, no caution, no nothing. Yes, it's close to home, yes, Iron Kettle and the Big Long Knife are enjoying each other, yes, the little Long Knife must spend all day looking at his—book, you call it?—but is stupid.

Is life so bad you want to give yours to the Siksikas? So must have a little fun, teach a little lesson.

"We compliment you on how fast you trail us, but running men cannot keep up with running horses. And we watch you every moment. No good to have you get lost and sacrifice your scalps to maybeso Shoshone children.

"When you sneak on camp, and wonder where our guard is, all five of us are behind you already, sneaky watching you." She slapped her thigh, laughing, and then snatched the wig from Hairy.

Pine Leaf took the wig and arranged it on Tal's head. She tilted her head back and forth to get him to model it. "Is very pretty," she declared, "I think I love you.

"Iron Kettle tells us about make-believe hair, so we make-believe scalp you. Hi-yi-yi!" She beamed at Hairy.

"You make it best—you fall in creek. Is wonderful, I salute you.

"We are victors," she said to boys, "we deserve trophy." She reached for Tal's rifle, drew it across her lap, and spread the silk handkerchief with her hands. "Very pretty," she said. She glanced wickedly at Tal. "Very easy to see from hill, so you make good target. I take it instead of scalp."

She untied the handkerchief quickly and retied it around one of her braids, looking mischievously at Tal. He was transfixed on the colors of fire and sky against her long, bare, soft-looking neck. "Now you are my captive."

She borrowed a mirror from Hairy and studied herself. "Very pretty," she cooed. "Maybe I trade you something for it later. Now maybeso I wear it."

"It's a gift," Tal murmured.

"No, no, Little Long Knife. No gift." she chuckled. "You make gift to Pine Leaf, Antelope Jim he make gloves from your hide." She wagged a long finger at him.

"Later," she said, "I decide what to give you for it."

Anything would have sufficed. For Tal was in love. He had a new lady as a shrine for his adventures.

And he wasn't afraid of no Antelope Jim Beckwourth.

10

Of fantasy, of dreams, and ceremonies
                                        —Julius Caesar II. i

Nothing was easier than getting Jim to tell stories.

He was brown as a roasted coffee bean, a strapping fellow, nearly as tall as Hairy and within a hundred pounds of the bulk—Hairy joked that Tal added on to Antelope Jim would make a Shakespeare.

In his stories Jim was a Gargantua. That's what Hairy called him. To everyone's surprise, Beckwourth answered with teasing formality, "Indeed I do have big appetites and no woman among the Crow people will say me nay—thus will the nation become populated with braver men of blacker faces."

Beckwourth could talk like an educated man because his father was one. Jim liked to say his father was an aristocratic Virginian who took his children, born into slavery, to St. Louis and raised them like they were free, white, and twenty-one.

But Jim certainly didn't mind his black face—black was what Crows painted themselves after a victory, so Jim looked like he was always a man to honor.

Jim was fonder of nothing more than an audience, especially an admiring one. Usually his stories were brags, but he could tell one on himself.

"I'd been hunting big horns," he launched into another one, "and stopped in at the lodge of my brother-friend to hint on how many I'd killed. 'Eat,' said my brother, and I set in. A man can't hardly go hungry around here." (That was a brag on the Absaroka people.)

"It was strips of buffalo tongue, which is always half raw, so I won't touch it. But this time his wife had put the flame to it good, and I helped myself heartily and then some. Wagh!

"When I'd finished, thought I'd maybeso have a little fun. Asked her what the meat was.

" 'Tongue,' she says odd-like, 'cause she knew I knew.

"I looked at my brother and rolled my eyes and grabbed my belly.

"Knowing I never ate tongue, he thought he took my meaning. 'Tongue,' he hollered. 'Tongue?! You've gone against Antelope's medicine. Oh, God, his medicine's ruined.'

"He was pretty near hysterical. 'If he dies in battle, you're a goner,' he moaned, pointing at her. He knew someone would give her the ax if her carelessness cost the people so great a warrior as me." Jim flashed his winning grin.

"She looked like she'd been axed already. Mouth gaping. Eyes rolling. Legs wobbling.

"This child got to his hands and knees and set in to beller like a buffler. I four-footed my way outside. I lolled my tongue out. I pawed the ground in my mighty anger.

"All this like I was trying to throw off the effect of eating the tongue and save my medicine.

"Naturally, I gathered a crowd. How they was worried! Wagh!"

When Jim made that sound, it didn't pop like when Hairy made it. It grumbled, like a belch.

"They took to wailing and lamenting the terrible accident. They sent a mighty sound unto the skies.

"Well, pretty soon I'd had my fun and strode along home to Still Water and thought no more about it." Still Water was his senior wife. "Ate hump ribs instead, and practiced making babies.

"But, coons, the great Coyote in the sky, he surprises us." Lacking God, Jim used Coyote.

"The very next day we had a buffalo surround, and discovered some Blackfeet forting up nearby. They was in for it, and they knew it. Well, I can't never help showing off, so first thing I ride like the devil himself right up to them and hit one with my coup stick for first coup." Jim grinned a braggart's grin at them— first coup was top coup, and to strike without injuring was the top of the top.

"Then this child rides off a little ways to watch the fun.

"Ka-a-a-boom! I'm whomped by something te-e-e-rrific in the belly and fall off my horse.

"I'm bleeding at the mouth. Naturally I think I'm gut-shot and give myself up to go under and let my friends carry me off.

"Lord, how the women did wail when they saw Antelope Jim struck down! This own child thought his medicine maybeso got spoiled.

"My brother's wife, she cried herself right onto her horse and hightailed it. She figured she wouldn't last the night. Left my brother-friend with no one to keep him warm.

"But when the medicine men checked me over, they just found a bruise. The bullet hadn't penetrated! 'A miracle! What medicine Antelope Jim has! His skin turns lead!'

"Later I found the flattened bullet in my scabbard, and the knife handle smashed." He held up a disc of lead hanging from his neck by a thong. He winked. "But I did not see fit to enlighten my comrades about the exact nature of my powerful medicine."

"My brother's wife went clear to the Missouri to live with the River Crows, and didn't come back until she saw me alive and well at the medicine lodge the next summer.

"I offered to loan him one of my wives for the winter," Jim said nonchalantly, "but he went dry instead."

Tal and Hairy had been extra welcome—these were people who knew how to make you feel like family. Iron Kettle's family, which was poor, even gave them a horse each—unbroke, true, but horseflesh just the same.

Right off Iron Kettle surprised them by moving into her sister's lodge, and avoiding Hairy. Tal didn't realize for a week that she'd become a second wife to her sister's husband. That's the way of it, Antelope Jim explained. If you lose your husband, your sister's husband takes you. Handy, said the big mulatto.

Beckwourth practically adopted them from the first day. Tal and Hairy pitched their lean-to (Hairy's lean-to, it was, actually) at a decent distance from camp, but Jim was over there all the time.

One night he arranged a sweat bath. Just to make us feel good, he said.

The helper kept bringing hot rocks into the low, hide-covered hut, and Jim would pour water on them from a kettle and fill the hut with steam. The heat was incredible. You'd lie in there, naked and perfectly silent, for maybe ten minutes and then slip out and gasp for breath like a beached fish in the chill night air. Hairy turned purple and stayed outside after the first round. Because Beckwourth teased Hairy about that, Tal stayed in for four full rounds, suffering grievously. Then Jim took a final round alone.

The mountain air felt delightful on Tal's baked skin. The night was clear and moonless. The stars shone with the brightness particular to mountain skies. Tal felt weak, and drained, and cuddly, and oddly affectionate toward Jim. He came out and joined them.

Hairy was dozing.

"We're maybeso friends now," said Jim. "So I give ye the right of a friend to ask me a personal question."

"Oh, I wouldn't do that," Tal demurred, hanging his head.

"Don't you want to be friends?"

"Sure, sure, but…" Hairy started to bugle, as Iron Kettle called it—he really did sound like an elk bugling, whether he was snoring or mating—and Jim slapped his foot. Hairy stopped.

"I'm going to ask you a personal question," Jim assured Tal. "Just one."

"Oh."

Hairy started to bugle again. Jim slapped him and he stopped.

"All right." Tal moved closer to the fire for heating the rocks. It was a windless night, but nippy.

Hairy bugled. Jim took the kettle and pitched the water on Hairy's face. Hairy sat up spluttering.

"Pay attention, Shakespeare," said Jim. "Tal's gonna tell us where he's from and about his folks." He turned to Tal. "That's my one question."

"He's told nothing but lies about that so far," mumbled Hairy.

"I know," Jim said softly. "Well, Tal?"

Hairy was right. Tal had a collection of inventions about his origins, performed according to occasion.

He told Cap'n Fitzpatrick that he'd run away from the blacksmith he was apprenticed to, on account of being beat on. In fact, that had happened to the youngster Tal signed on for Santa Fe with, not to Tal. One of his favorites was a whopper about being the run-away son of a St. Louis slaveholder—he run away 'cause human beings ought not to be owned by anybody, but his pa whipped him for saying so. He also had a couple of well-practiced stories about being on the lam from the law.

Then, yesterday, he'd told Jim and Pine Leaf one about coming from a family of musicians who hailed from Montreal. Poverty-stricken, they were, but the joy of music resided in them. Only Tal was tone deaf, and got left out, so he had to skeedaddle.

He thought it was a pretty story at the time, appealing and with a touch of pathos.

"Tal?"

Tal wondered why he liked to befog his origins. He wasn't sure he wanted to know. So he shrugged and started on the mundane truth.

"My dad was a preacher. His family had been in the mines. In Wales. They come—came," Tal corrected himself, "here to try to do better when he was a boy. Dad got the call to spread the Gospel. He meant it, my dad—the Gospel was his life—God, poetry, and music."

Jim draped a blanket around Tal's shoulders, and he snuggled into it. He felt a kind of magic in the night, the fire, the camaraderie.

"Dad wandered. Wandered all over the East, preaching to those that would listen, living by passing the hat, and what lessons he would give. He taught reading and writing where he could, and singing. Mostly used John Milton and John Bunyan, *Paradise Lost* and *Pilgrim's Progress,* the two divine books in the English language, he called them."

Tal flashed a smart-aleck grin. "I can't stand to hear either one of them anymore. Well, I can but I can't."

He stared into the flames and drifted back into remembering. "Dad had a hard time of it, I guess. All he had in this world was a love of God, an ear for music and poetry, and a lovely tenor voice. Went from place to place, moving on when the hat came back empty."

Tal got quiet a while. "Once he moved on just ahead of the sheriff. Got too friendly with another man's wife. That's how I came along." He looked challengingly at his two friends.

"Mom followed him to St. Louis, where my aunt, his sister, was living. I was born there. Mom stuck it out, for a while. Then we never saw her again.

"That's when he started drinking. Not bad, but enough. I tried to keep it from the congregation, but I couldn't. At first they felt for him and tried to help him back into the fold. After a while they gave up.

"I did too. I'd been working at the mercantile and playing clavichord at church and dad was keeping us both broke with the spirits. One night I told him that

God and Jesus were just stories, like St. Nick, stories for kids. Which is the truth.

"We had a fight. With fists. He hit me, but he'd done that before."

Tal was quiet for a moment. "I hit him. First time. Scared both of us." He let out a long sigh. "I ran off. Crying. I was just a kid. Stayed gone, sleeping in alleys.

"The second week I went home for my clothes and he was gone. Neighbors said they thought he'd gone to the mountains. General Ashley told me Dad had signed on with the rendezvous caravan as a clerk.

"He'd left the family Bible for me, and a message in it: 'I can help you no more, son. My legacy to you is your love of music, which is the sound of divinity on earth. I hope you, unlike your father, can stay off the spirits.'"

Tal took a long breath, looked at them naked, and then turned his face away. "Nobody out here remembers Dad. Maybe he went under," he murmured. "But I'd know it. I'd know if Dad didn't walk the earth."

Beckwourth let the silence be. Hairy was staring off into the darkness.

After a long while, Jim said, "I love music, too."

They let this remark sit in the still night air.

Then Antelope Jim Beckwourth, mulatto, lifted his rough, grainy baritone into the night sky with his favorite hymn:

I am a poor, wayfaring stranger,
A-trav'ling through this land of woe,
It was in a minor key, plaintive and forlorn.

But there's no trouble, no toil or danger
In that bright land to which I go.
In a moment Hairy's resonant basso joined in. And Tal, teary-eyed, added his frail, reedy sound.
(chorus)
I'm going home to see my father,
I'm going home no more to roam.
I'm just a-going over Jordan.
I'm just a-going over home.
They sat and gazed into the flames, each man alone with his mortality, while the echoes of the old hymn died away.

Full fathom five thy father lies,
Hairy broke the silence, and rumbled on,
Of his bones are...
Tal gave him a look that had the smell of burnt gunpowder, and Hairy stopped.

Jim put a hand on Hairy's shoulder. "Long as we're doing the truth," he rasped at Hairy, "what about your parents?"

"My humble origins?"

Jim nodded.

"My father loved me, but couldn't take care of me. My, how he doted on me. Sent my sister back across the water to her aunt, but he tried to keep me with him. When I was five, he had to leave me in care of the nuns in Philadelphia. He took to the road again to make our fortune. He was an actor"—Hairy always made the last syllable rhyme with *oar*—"had been in a company in Leeds and always yearned to go back, back to the land of Shakespeare and Milton, back where the sound of the English language swells and roars like the surf on the rocks…"

Jim pushed Hairy over, almost into the fire.

"Shakespeare didn't sweat enough to get the fabrications out of him," Antelope Jim said, chuckling.

"Life itself is a fabrication," said Hairy, "a figment of the imagination of the Creator." Hairy gave Jim his toothiest grin. "He was having an excess of creativity when he dreamed you up."

Jim rewarded Hairy with a smile and turned to Tal. "Now maybeso you'd like to ask your one personal question."

Tal fussed with his fingers and wriggled his toes. "Don't have none," he mumbled.

"Isn't something on your mind about me and Pine Leaf?"

Tal pondered a moment, then stammered, "Well, is it true you want her for, uh, another wife?"

Jim grinned toothily.

"Yup," he said easily, "she's my sort of woman. Asked her to marry me three autumns ago when we were going against some Assiniboins on the Milk River. If both of us came out of it alive, I said. Truth was, I didn't think we would come out of it alive. We hollered, 'It's a good day to die!' and rode on. And here we are.

"Know what she said?"

"Nope." Tal was popping his knuckles.

"Looked me full in the eye, and said gravely, 'Yes, I will marry you, Antelope Jim. Not now, but when the pine leaves turn yellow.'

"Wagh! My eyes near overflowed, and I rode into that fight half blind. Fought like a demon, so I could stay on earth till Pine Leaf was my woman. I was a dust devil that day, everywhere at once, elusive as the wind.

"Wasn't till that evening when I thought, pine leaves don't turn color. Ever.

"Pine Leaf was taking a doze. I shook her awake. Says I, 'But pine leaves don't turn yellow.'

"Her eyes laughed a little. 'I know,' says she.

"Then when will you marry me?"

" 'When you find a red-headed Indian,' she says, and turns over and pretends to be asleep."

Jim looked Tal full in the face. "So I guess that means never. Though I ain't sure. Half the people in the tribe think she'll come to me. She just likes making me wait.

"But I am sure she better not marry anybody else, 'cause this child will make that nigger into a steer." And he gave his fine, immense, malicious smile.

Hairy was covering himself with a blanket, too. Only Jim remained naked. The sky was turning iridescent pink in the east.

There was a soft sound, a clearing of the throat.

Pine Leaf stood behind them. She'd walked softly up through the trees without Tal noticing.

Jim seemed to radiate nakedness. Tal huddled tighter in his blanket. Hairy was bugling lightly again.

Pine Leaf smiled, and it made her face gorgeous in the sunrise. She took Tal's breath away.

She sat down between Tal and Jim. She was wearing his silk handkerchief in her hair, as always. Color of fire, color of sky, he thought proudly—House of Jones.

"What you been talking about, women? All three"—she said a word Tal didn't understand—"are you?"

"Horny," Beckwourth translated.

"Antelope Jim says you won't marry him until the pine leaves turn yellow, or he finds a red-headed Indian," Tal put in boldly, like he was teasing.

"True," said Pine Leaf. "That is for him. For every other horny man—they all want Pine Leaf, so they can maybe so send her to war for them and save their own scalps—I have made a different condition.

"Someone must bring me Leg-in-the-Water's war horse. But not one of them has the courage to get it."

11

If music be the food of love, play on
—Twelfth Night, I.i

It was true.

Pine Leaf had told half a dozen Crow men that she would marry them if they brought her the horse that Leg-in-the-Water, chief of the Cheyennes, used in battle. Tal found that out from Yellow Foot, one of Pine Leaf's suitors. Everyone knew the horse, a big sorrel that Leg-in-the-Water always kept staked by his lodge. Almost every day he renewed the medicine painting on the horse, a hand on the neck and a ring around one eye.

"You'll see the horse at Fort Cass," said Yellow Foot. He was a slender young man with skin smooth as a girl's and a languid way about him. "Leg-in-the-Water likes to camp by the fort for a while in the fall. It's an ordinary looking horse, but brave in the charge."

Leg-in-the-Water cherished that horse. To steal it would be to wound the entire Cheyenne nation. And win hosannahs from the entire Crow nation.

But who could steal a horse tied by the lodge skirts of its owner, in the middle of a village of hundreds of watchers and listeners? So Yellow Foot, leaving Tal and Hairy's fire for his own lodge, asked rhetorically.

Watching the embers die, Tal thought on it and judged he could. He thought. Maybe. At the risk of a tail full of arrows.

He'd need Hairy's help. He looked at Hairy dozing, and bugling, in the lean-to. Hairy would go along if the plan sounded a little crazy and a lot of fun. Sure, Hairy was his partner.

Tal mulled on a plan while the three were out trapping.

They had to take at least some beaver, Jim insisted. Otherwise, how would they get powder and ball, much less the baubles that the women like, from the trader at the fort? Hairy didn't want to trap. He could get a bale of plews, he said, playing the shell game with the Crows. (He had a walnut shell that nearly matched his ruined fingernail, promoting confusion.) Stalking the big water rats, in Hairy's opinion, was unseemly.

Jim gave him a nasty look. "You'd best ease off tricking your hosts," he commented. Hairy had been using the shell game, and his skill at ventriloquism, and even an occasional spot of mesmerism to build his reputation and fatten his purse. "Besides," said Jim, "I'm on salary."

"On *what?*" said Tal.

"Salary from American Fur," Jim allowed. "This child lets the company pay him for making sure the trade of the Absaroka people goes to American Fur, and not Rocky Mountain Fur. So he's obliged to set an example and trap a few beaver."

These were the two substantial firms of the mountains and plains, not counting the Britishers over to Oregon. Rocky Mountain Fur was the outfit Fitzpatrick and Frapp were partners of. American Fur was owned by John Jacob Astor and some rich French families in St. Louis.

"The tribe will go down in about a month," said Jim. "And you coons absolutely got no plews to trade, like this nigger."

So Tal and Hairy and Jim worked both forks of the Stinking Water, taking beaver aplenty. They went without Pine Leaf, who disdained such working for the white man.

" 'Put money in thy purse,' " Hairy recited sententiously, "quoth the immortal Iago."

They did. They had an excellent month. Meanwhile Tal was raising his courage about that horse.

They couldn't tell Antelope Jim, Tal and Hairy agreed, because he'd either squash the adventure or insist on coming along.

And they couldn't steal the horse by the fort, where both tribes would be camped. By custom the fort was neutral territory. But they could sneak off from the tribe and follow the Cheyennes and...

"And do what comes naturally," Hairy said mischievously, like a three-hundred-pound imp.

It almost misfired.

The Crows were late getting down to Fort Cass that year, and as they came over Pryor's Gap, the Cheyennes were packing up to head back to their wintering quarters.

Tal got all roiled when he heard. Hairy went to Yellow Foot and offered him something nice to help out. Hairy would give Yellow Foot a nice tin of ochre paint, he said, if Yellow Foot would ride with them and point out Leg-in-the-Water and his war horse, and not give away their intention. Hairy showed Yellow Foot the little tins of greasepaint he kept from his acting days, every color in the rainbow. Afterwards Hairy laughed and told Tal he could have gotten a wife for each tin, Yellow Foot was so fascinated.

The identification was no trouble. The huge Cheyenne village rode down the Yellowstone Valley openly—warriors at both ends, women and children in the middle with travois laden with trade goods, dogs romping and yapping everywhere. Yellow Foot led Tal and Hairy to a knoll where they could see the entire procession. Leg-in-the-Water was toward the front with other members of his warrior club. He rode a paint and led a big sorrel.

Tal feasted his eyes on the horse, and studied it in his spyglass. Leg-in-the-Water himself was an unimpressive-looking Indian.

"His tomahawk will make an impression on your head if you don't watch out," Yellow Foot said as they rode back. He said it idly, gently, in his fashion. Tal liked Yellow Foot and his doe-eyed style and strange, giddy sense of humor. Antelope Jim, Yellow Foot's particular friend, said Yellow Foot wanted to marry Pine Leaf and to become chief after Rotten Belly. Despite Yellow Foot's gentle ways, said Jim, he was a man to be reckoned with.

Back to the fort they went. Tal hated the delay, but Hairy pointed out that the village would be easy to follow, and the Cheyennes would keep a particularly careful watch until they got further from the Crows.

"Bide your time," said Hairy. "That's the mark of the hunter."

So they traded. Tal didn't want anything but enough of DuPont's powder to fill two horns and some Galena lead for balls. He didn't like all the foofooraw the trader got the Indians' plews with—bells, mirrors, vermilion, blue cloth and red, bolts of silk (very expensive), combs, and beads of every description. Tal didn't mean to go courting with gee-gaws but a fine stolen horse.

Tal traded his extra plews to Jim for another pack horse. Jim had plenty of horse flesh, dozens of animals, and pointed out that Tal was a poor man in the mountains indeed, with only one horse and one mule. Tal wished he was mountain-rich enough for a buffalo runner or a war horse, but...Rosie was a comfortable old shoe.

He would have bought Pine Leaf something nice, but she insisted she wanted nothing. She did wear Tal's silk handkerchief, his coat of arms, in her hair every day, and said that was plenty foofooraw for her. She wrapped a *taja* around Tal's waist and exclaimed how smart it looked. It was a woven sash the Spaniards wore for dress-up. Tal flushed and studied himself in the mirror but allowed as how he had better things to spend his plews on.

It was tempting, though. Robert the Bruce and Launcelot and Don Quixote and such like-probably put on the dog. Hairy said they even wore tights, and pulled a pair out of his theatrical trunk to show.

Tal decided he'd get a sash some day, and a pleated shirt, too, for showy occasions, but the idea of tights made him blush.

Hairy was a crafty trader. He resupplied his firearms readily enough, but did a lot of talking with Mr. Tulloch, the head man, about what else he wanted. Then he went back to camp and traded with Yellow Foot for a war club—a heavy cudgel-like affair with a spike, lifted from a scalped Blackfoot. Hairy seemed quite pleased with that. Then he lazed a while, and went back to haggle with Tulloch twice more. Before finally striking his deal, he got Tulloch to indulge in a game of chance for the final haggling margin. Naturally, Hairy won.

He didn't show everything, but Tal saw he got a nice bagful of pony beads, a fill-up for his whisky keg, and a small keg of powder. For some reason Hairy seemed unreasonably pleased with that keg.

Tal went up on the ramparts, where he could gaze outside the stockade across the whole vista of the valley of the Yellowstone, a sweep of plains framed by distant blue mountains. The Crow camp was in the near distance, by the cottonwoods near the river. Hide lodges pointed at the sky. Indian braves strolled in skin clothing ornamented by feathers, ermine tails, porcupine quill-work, and scalps. Squaws tended fires cooking buffalo roasts and tongues. It had grandeur. It had romance.

He thrilled at himself, Tal Jones of St. Louis, plain old Missouri, dwelling among these splendid barbarians as one of them, living a life of heroic legend. He stuck his hand in his shot pouch to feel for the grizzly claws lying in there, his first trophies.

"Hoss?"

It was Antelope Jim's voice. He was on the ladder. Tal motioned him up. "Didn't want to disturb your reverie," Jim allowed. He was holding something behind his back.

"Grand, ain't it, Jim?"

Jim looked around at the plains and the mountains and the camp and smiled handsomely. "It be, hoss, it be.

"Got something for you." Jim held out a long, slender shape wrapped in deerskin. "Open it."

Tal unfolded the skin and beheld...a sort of flute, it looked like. It was made from two pieces of wood hollowed and glued together, and decorated with small carvings of animals and an eagle feather. The mouthpiece was shaped like a bird's head.

Tal stuck it in his mouth, got a nod from Jim, and blew. It made an eerie sound in the emptiness of the evening. Finger holes gave him different tones, a full scale, but the pitch wobbled plaintively.

Touched, he smiled shyly at Jim.

"It's a maverick kind of flute," Jim explained. "Tulloch's daughter Ginny made it, looking like what the Sioux make, but sounding like what white folks make. Ginny's a breed, and gets her kinds of music confused. I traded old Tulloch out of it."

"What's Ginny like?"

"Pretty girl, 'bout your age."

"Maybe she'll teach me to play it."

"May be, but she's off with her mother's folks now. You maybeso can teach yourself. This child would cotton to a little music around the camp fire."

Tal blew a few notes melismatically—forlorn, sad notes they seemed in the Western twilight.

"Thanks," said Tal, and rubbed the wood.

"You're welcome, hoss. Truth is, I thought your daddy would like you to have a flute, mountain-style, to make praises to Coyote on." And Jim circled his shoulders with a big arm.

12

to feats of broil and battle

—Othello, I.iii

Fortune and destiny were with them.

Leg-in-the Water had told Mr. Tulloch, said the trader, that the Cheyennes would winter on Powder River. But the season was early, the start of November, Tulloch pointed out, so they still might break up to hunt first. When the Cheyennes headed east, Tal and Hairy lazed two days, promised Jim and Pine Leaf to see them back at the forks of the Stinking Water, and set out on their adventure. Their first real escapade, Tal thought.

In half the night plus half a day they caught up with the main body. They watched through the spyglass, and waited.

They were glassing from a couple of miles back when their quarry split off from the main group and headed up the Tongue River. A dozen lodges went along. Tal had eyes for nothing but that horse. Leg-in-the-Water never let go its lead rope.

The two cut across and struck the valley of the Tongue well ahead, keeping to the high hills bordering the river valley, three or four miles in front.

"Don't want the scouts to pick us up," Hairy said. "That lot will scout well."

Tal thought they'd size things up for a couple of days and then make their move.

"Nay, lad," rumbled Hairy, "we'll not play Hamlet. Away with doubt. We strike tonight."

"All right, jolly," murmured Tal, "let's do it."

The Indians made camp at mid-afternoon in a wide meadow by the river, among some tall, dead-leaved cotton-woods.

Tal and Hairy hid their own horses in a thick grove about a mile upstream and lay quiet in some rocks and watched, alternating with the spyglass.

The horse was hobbled with others in some good grass a hundred yards from camp, under guard. Not long before sunset Leg-in-the-Water himself brought the horse in and picketed it next to his lodge. The day was getting cool, and smoke rose from the lodge flaps.

Your dinner and a warm fire, Leg-in-the-Water, thought Tal, while I am cold and have to eat pemmican. After tonight you are a dishonored man.

The plan was easy. They'd walk from here—couldn't risk a whicker from the horses. Hairy would take out the pony guard. Tal would sneak in, pull the picket, and bridle the horse right off. Then lead it ever so gently out of camp. That would make a certain amount of noise—perhaps the Cheyennes would sleep through it or ignore it. If not, Tal could jump on the horse and be gone into the dark before anyone could bother him. Once the horse was bridled—that was the key.

And maybe Hairy would spook the entire pony herd, just to keep the Cheyennes off their trail.

In any case the two would meet back at their horses and travel all night.

"She's a mite tricky, lad, but she should come out." He looked sharp at Tal. "Faint heart never won fair maiden."

True enough. Tal wanted that horse. There was nothing to do now but wait. And wait.

Tal fished in his possible sack and came out with his flute.

Hairy fished in his and came out with actor's paints, red, white, and black. He took off his shirt, exposing sheet-white belly and back and arms.

Tal dared not actually play the flute, for fear of the sound's carrying to enemies. He hummed a fast, tricky tune and practiced fingering it on the instrument.

"That's a love flute, you know," Hairy said. He was spreading white paint all over his front, liberally. It made him gleam.

"A *love* flute?"

"Yeah, the Sioux claim one of those will charm a girl right out of her drawers. No sense in trying to resist one of those, Sioux women say."

Tal looked at it anew. Could he charm Pine Leaf with this? Would he need to, once he stole

Leg-in-the-Water's war horse? "Won't fetch the warrior woman, this child don't believe," Hairy put in, reading Tal's mind.

Tal flushed. "How come?"

"It's Sioux, for one thing, not Crow. Medicine to the goose may be p'isen to the gander. For another thing, it was made by Ginny, and not by a medicine man, as should be. And if it had the medicine for Pine Leaf, Antelope Jim would have used it his own self."

Tal wrinkled his nose.

Hairy took off his pants and started rubbing his legs shiny white.

"Also," Hairy went on, "it makes white-man notes, not red-man notes."

Hairy now was finger-painting vertical black stripes from head to toe.

Trying to finger the flute and figure what the heck Hairy was doing, Tal was getting flustered. He decided to pay Hairy no mind.

"What's Ginny like?" Tal asked casually.

Hairy smiled, thinking back. "'Bout your age, I guess. A year ago she was built like a willow, but coming graceful like a woman. And inde-e-ependent? That girl don't pay her father no attention."

"How would I charm a girl, if I wanted to?" Tal asked.

"The way it works, you get the flute and a song at the same time from a medicine man. Trade for them. Costs handsome 'cause it's powerful. Then you play the song, and the girl melts." Hairy made his ogre grin.

"The warrior woman didn't actual promise *you* to marry if you got the horse, did she?"

"No," Tal said softly.

"I wouldn't count on the flute, lad. And I don't believe the lady has eyes for you."

Tal knew Hairy thought that. So did Antelope Jim. And Yellow Foot and the rest. They didn't take his courtship seriously, on account of he was young.

But Tal thought different. He thought Pine Leaf was interested. Why else would she always dally and talk to him? What did it mean that she always wore the blazon of the House of Jones, the color of fire and the color of sky? Maybe she was going to fool them all. So it was up to Tal to make bold and ask for her hand.

Hairy had taken off his wig and was rubbing the top of his head scarlet. He reddened his stub of ear, too.

Tal resolved to pay him no mind. He fingered a song of love, and hummed it to Pine Leaf, his inamorata.

It was cussedly light. The moon was flooding the grass and lodges and trees and river bright enough to read, nearly. Tal could see Hairy plainly, down to a gleam on the spike of his war club. Hairy was creeping, one careful step at a time, back from the station of the pony guard. At least that must have gone well. Tal hadn't heard a thing, and Hairy was coming back alive.

Tal was darn irked at Hairy. Besides putting on that body paint, he'd smeared his face white as linen and put on a white fright wig. Above his dark blanket, under which he wore nothing, his face shone like a shaggy moon.

"Magic," Hairy had said. "Power."

Something other than magic, too—Hairy was hiding something under the blanket.

Tal wasn't going to let Hairy's antics stop him. He'd blacked his face and hands, to be less visible.

Hairy motioned forward with a hand, and Tal moved out. He walked silently but quickly—there was no cover from here to the camp. It was three or four o'clock in the morning, so everyone should be asleep.

Near the first lodge he circled a little back toward the hill and went into a clump of boulders and stood perfectly still in the shadow of the big one, watching. His heart was thumping like a bird's.

He could see Leg-in-the-Water's lodge in front of the big cottonwood, and the horse on the left of the door flap. Leg-in-the-Water and his woman were asleep inside, alone.

No movement in camp, and not a sound.

What?

A human shape pitched off the boulder above, and flumped onto the ground.

Hairy followed it, landing astride the shape with surprising agility. His knife slid into the throat in the motion of the jump.

Tal thought he was going to scream and wet his pants at once.

Tal looked up at the top of the boulder, and realized that the Cheyenne must have been there about to leap on him, and Hairy spotted it and...

Hairy stood up right in front of Tal, grinning lewdly at him. Hairy was now stark naked, glowing white with black stripes all over, even on his...thing.

Tal put a finger to the corner of his mouth, then realized that the finger was his knife and he'd cut himself.

Lordgodawmighty, let's git before us fools get killed.

Hairy pushed Tal forward.

Tal started to whirl and use the knife on Hairy. He got hold of himself. All right, he would....Step by careful step, Tal moved past one, two, three, four lodges, avoiding various ropes and poles.

He kept his eye on the horse. His main fear was that the beast would see them coming and make some sort of noise. He had a sudden fantasy of the horse flying to the top of the lodge and blowing the Judgment Day trumpet.

He didn't hesitate, didn't slow down, just moved quietly up to the horse. The animal was watching him.

Dad, what did I do to get here? He reached out and put his lead rope around the horse's neck. No blare of trumpet. He was just getting the bridle on when the door flap scratched and opened.

Leg-in-the-Water himself stepped out. Naked.

Tal was crouched under the horse, clutching the lead rope.

Leg-in-the-Water stepped aside and started pissing.

A hand touched Tal's shoulder. He wet his pants.

Hairy. Hairy's hand, and Hairy's face.

The face glowed in the moonlight. This goddam moonface is going to get us both killed, thought Tal.

Lord. Stark naked, painted glow-worm-white and crazy-black all over.

Leg-in-the-Water's stream sound was slowing down.

Hairy moved swiftly around the horse. Rose. Raised the war club. Lunged. Slammed Leg-in-the-Water in the back of the skull.

Leg-in-the-Water fell like broken reeds. Hairy eased his way to the ground.

The blow had sounded loud.

Words came from the lodge. A woman's voice, Cheyenne words.

Hairy grunted.

Tal squeezed the lead rope harder and tried to disappear into the ground. The horse was getting restless, moving its feet.

Hairy started pissing on the ground. Good thinking, Hairy!

The horse started pissing on Tal's back. Tal jumped out of the way. The horse piss made a fine, loud sound.

A grunt came from the lodge.

Hairy switched his stream to Leg-in-the-Water's body.

When Hairy drew his scalping knife and bent over the dead form, Tal fastened the bridle and started out. Fast. He was struggling not to run.

The horse's hoofbeats sounded like drumbeats to Tal, but he kept walking back the way he came.

At the edge of camp he slipped up onto the horse and guided it toward the pony herd.

Suddenly he felt his heart bumpety-bumping again, and warm tears filled his eyes.

Tears of what? Heck, he didn't know. He was soaked with horse piss. And his own piss. But he had Leg-in-the-Water's war horse.

No sign of Hairy behind him, or of fifty warriors behind Hairy.

He tied the horse to a tree and checked the priming on rifle and pistol.

He waited. No sign of Hairy.

Well, Tal couldn't bear to wait.

He moved quietly back toward camp. Past the herd. Past the first lodges. Into the clump of boulders. Past the body of the Cheyenne, now scalped. Up the big boulder. He sat on Hairy's unfolded blanket, to see.

Just then Leg-in-the-Water's lodge lit up like a candle, and burst into flame.

Hairy busted out of the lodge. He was carrying a woman. Laid her on the ground clear of the burning lodge next to Leg-in-the-Water. Then sprinted toward the boulders.

In the shadow of Tal's boulder Hairy picked up his rifle. Godawmighty, thought Tal.

Hairy was kneeling and checking his prime.

No need to worry about being heard now. The fire was roaring, and shouts and calls were coming from all over camp. "Hi, Hairy," Tal said mockingly.

"Thought you might come back, hoss," said Hairy without looking up. "Now's the fun."

Indians were running toward the burning lodge and tree, exclaiming, hurrying back and forth. Some stamped out burning grass. Some stood over the prone figures of Leg-in-the-Water and his woman. Clearly it was too late to do anything for the lodge, and it looked like the fire would not spread much. Wails and cries of grief went up.

In the distance the horses were nickering and milling.

"Ain't she fine, lad, ain't she fine?" Hairy seemed transfixed by the blaze.

"What are you doing, Hairy?" Tal whispered urgently.

"Gathering me a crowd, lad." Hairy lifted his rifle.

He had a crowd all right, three dozen men and a dozen women, two or three of them holding small children. Two women were trying to bring the unconscious squaw around.

"Look at the crotch of the tree."

Tal couldn't make out anything but a red spot, like a glowing coal. "What was in the blanket?" he asked nervously.

"We're gonna have us a spectacle," Hairy sang.

Then came God's own thunder.

The loudest sound Tal had ever heard.

A flash of light that left him blind for a moment.

The dry-leaved cottonwood went up like a torch.

People backed away, or fell on the ground, their arms raised.

Hairy was reloading calmly. "A powder keg has its uses, lad," he said lightly. "Ain't she fine?" He gazed at the torch, a half-mad gleam in his eyes.

A chorus of screams and wails, as from the maw of hell.

"Scared more than hurt," Hairy went on. "Surely does take the fight out of them, though."

One Indian was running up to the wailing crowd, priming his gun. Hairy shot him and laid the rifle down.

He looked up at Tal. "Now's the time to spook the herd, lad. Not that they'll need much spooking. Wait for me at camp."

Pistol in one hand, war club in the other, Hairy ran toward the crowd. He was bellowing a war-cry and whirling the club over his head.

In the tree-torchlight, naked and painted insanely, roaring like a ghostly griz, brandishing his club, Hairy looked like every man's nightmare of death.

Any Cheyenne able to use his feet, or hands and knees, got up on them. Hairy whirled like a dervish. He reached to his own head and ripped off the fright wig and waved it. His scalp was painted red.

Half the remaining Indians ran, screaming in panic.

Hairy issued a long, cackling scream of triumph. The others scattered like leaves in the wind.

Hairy was standing alone and naked. He began to laugh. He bubbled with laughter. He roared with laughter, a gargantuan clown.

Bewildered and elated, Tal started for the pony herd, wobbling as he ran.

13

excellent plot, very good friends
—Henry IV, Part 1, II.iii

They moved far and fast. Hairy insisted, though, that the chance of being followed was slim as a hair. This was meant as a tribute to his achievement, which he referred to as the rout of the Cheyenne nation.

"They shall long remember," Hairy gloated, "the mighty magic of Shakespeare. They shall relate in story and in song how they quaked in their boots before the tree that burst into a torch."

As a courtesy to Pine Leaf, Tal didn't ride her new war horse on the way. He was moody. He didn't feel like talking. Occasionally Hairy would slow down his whooping celebration to ask how come Tal had got sullen.

Sullen, yeah, that was it—he felt sullen.

How come? he wondered. Didn't I get the war horse, like I went for? Still, he was moody, and didn't care who knew it.

They got to winter camp on the evening of the third day. The people left their cooking fires and watched and gave ululations of joy as the two rode into camp. Hairy held up the bushy, red-black scalps, and Tal trailed the war horse.

Tal and Hairy had painted their faces black. The eyes of the women shone with admiration and gratitude. The men were beaming with pride. Beckwourth followed the two through camp, gesturing at them and repeating over and over in the Absaroka language the same words. Tal imagined he was saying over and over, "My friends," or "My brothers."

Welcome home, thought Tal. A sort of home. No, my legendary home, he told himself, my mountain aerie. He half-believed it.

Only Pine Leaf did not come out to welcome the two heroes.

Watching and listening to Hairy, Tal was irked—half at himself for telling his part too simply, too modestly, and half at Hairy for his braggadocio.

Antelope Jim had explained to Tal beforehand that this sort of celebration, coup-counting, was not bragging at all. It was carried on in a different style entirely from the white style—anyone who spoke was taking upon himself to tell the most particular and scrupulous truth, omitting interpretation and exaggeration and simply telling what he saw, no matter who looked good or bad. You were on your honor not to tell stretchers.

And Tal had told—how he took a notion from Pine Leaf's remark, though in truth she'd made no such promise to him. How they got Yellow Belly to point out the horse and the owner. How they'd followed the Cheyennes, and then just the band, on up the Tongue River. Exactly what they'd planned and exactly what they'd done. He was careful to give credit to Hairy for saving his life. Tal even included getting pissed on by the horse.

He'd quit with the part about getting the horse out of camp, because that was the end of his doings.

It wasn't till he was finished with the telling that he saw Pine Leaf sitting quietly at the back of a group of women. She surprised Tal with her gravity. He'd never seen her without a hint of devilment. Now she was simplicity, attention, respect. Tal figured he should feel complimented.

Hairy also told the truth accurately, but he made it a show. He spoke theatrically. He grinned and grimaced, gestured with his hands, used a little body English to enhance a point.

The Crows loved it, evidently, especially the women. Which is what irked Tal.

"Tal didn't know what devastation I truly had planned," Hairy explained. "I traded Tulloch for some linseed oil and a keg of powder. Wanted to get a show going. Nothing distracts people, or horses, like a fire. Nothing we needed more than a little distraction.

"After I scalped Leg-in-the-Water"—he paused for the cries of joy, and encouraged them by pumping one arm into the air—"I slipped into the lodge. Figured his woman couldn't tell between us in the dark.

"Knocked her on the head. Then had plenty of time in there all alone. Poured the oil all over everything.

Got the blaze going with a stub of candle—it went up fine. Hauled the woman out of there.

"Stowed the powder keg in the crotch of the tree, lit a slow fuse, and cleared off to watch the fun. Found Tal come back to help me, like a brave lad.

"Lodge blaze drew a crowd, she did. They was hollering on account of finding Leg-in-the-Water dead, and his woman out cold, and their lodge destroyed. All by an unseen enemy!" Hairy swaggered, practically waggling his tail.

"That's when I struck my real coup.

"When they was all there, ghoulish curious, the powder keg blew. Whooee! She blew!"

Cries of trepidation.

"The tree was all dead leaves, which lit up like candles. A sun in the night, we had, surrounded by many stars. The Cheyennes were staggered, struck in their hearts with fear. Such as were not knocked down, fled for their lives."

Cries of joy! Cries of victory!

Then Hairy told about shooting the one, and scalping him, showing the actual hair.

Tal still thought scalping was revolting. He could see, though, it was a crowd-pleaser.

The drums started, calling for the main event. Tal, uncertain now, stepped aside to get the object of his quest, Leg-in-the-Water's horse.

As Tal led the horse into the circle, Antelope Jim stepped close. Jim had the darnedest queer expression on his face.

"Give it to her proud, Tal," Beckwourth murmured. Yes, proud. So why did Jim look so sad? Oh. Maybe he feared he'd lost Pine Leaf.

Tal took a deep breath and stepped right out into the middle, near the fire. Little cries rose, and the drums stopped.

The horse looked splendid. Tal had curried it to a fine gloss, and tied Leg-in-the-Water's scalp in its red mane.

Tal looked around for Pine Leaf, and beckoned her forward. He seemed to have no words. When she came in front of him, he just handed her the lead rope. Then he remembered not to let his head hang, and lifted it proud.

Pine Leaf looked straight and deep into his eyes. She began to speak oratorically in the Absaroka language.

Antelope Jim, squatting behind Tal, translated softly:

"I thank my friend Tal for this fine horse, and Hairy for the scalp of its owner. They took great risk to get these prizes, and tricked the Cheyennes cleverly. I will be proud to ride the horse, and hope to honor Tal by killing many Blackfeet from its back."

Tal now understood the saying, it was worth it.

"I must tell them, though, that this is not Leg-in-the-Water's war horse, and the Cheyenne Shakespeare killed and scalped was not Leg-in-the-Water."

14

What's in a name?

—Romeo and Juliet, II.ii

Tal rocked on his feet, afraid of falling.

The people were hushed.

Antelope Jim stood up and said, "It's my fault."

Hairy pawed toward Jim, head down.

Yellow Foot stepped forward and spoke quickly in Absaroka. "I tell them," he repeated in English, "The fault is of me."

Hairy turned toward Yellow Foot, then toward Jim. He looked like a bull deciding which man to charge.

Yellow Foot continued, and Jim told the white men what he said. "When Tal said he wanted to steal the horse Pine Leaf had spoken of, I told Pine Leaf and we agreed that Leg-in-the-Water was too formidable an opponent.

"We spoke to Antelope."

"I said," put in Antelope Jim, chuckling, "that I didn't want these brave white men to take out our only worthy enemy among the Cheyennes." Laughter among the watchers.

"So we played a small trick on our friends," Yellow Foot went on. "I pointed out the wrong warrior to them, who had another fine sorrel horse."

A chorus of low exclamations from the people, mixed with smiles.

"I thought to protect them. I did not know they would prove so clever and so fierce. I am glad they are our friends, and ashamed to have deceived them."

Yellow Foot lifted his eyes to Hairy and Tal.

"To make up a little for my bad mistake, I have put ten ponies of my own by their lean-to, all fine ponies.

"I beg their forgiveness."

Yellow Foot hung his head.

Tal, swimming in a sea of strange feelings, stepped forward, grabbed Yellow Foot's hand, and shook it. Then he ran off into the dark.

Jim found him in the lean-to. Tal was trying to read *Scottish Chiefs* by candle lantern, but couldn't keep his mind on it.

Jim suggested they water the new horses, who were in a rope corral nearby. The two walked the dozen steps to the creek and back a few times, giving the animals water from their hats, not talking.

When they'd finished, Jim said, "Those are good horses. Extra good horses. Yellow Foot feels bad about what he done."

"Yeah," said Tal.

"He means to give you somep'n bigger'n horses."

Tal just stared at the ground.

"Means to protect your tail come spring. You see, come spring, whole lot of Cheyennes gonna be after your hair. And Hairy's more so. You boys plain embarrassed them."

Tal couldn't think what to make of this.

"You're gonna need friends," Jim added, "and you got em.

Tal scratched at the ground with one foot, then nodded.

"Best come back to the dance," Jim suggested. "Somep'n more's gonna happen for you. Somep'n nice."

They moved off together. "Hairy's already got what he wanted," Jim said, with a lewd smile. "Off in the bushes. He could get plenty of it tonight."

"When he gets a Crow name," Tal ventured, "it will be Mighty Mating."

"Don't tell my wives that," said Jim, tickled.

They were approaching the dancers around the fire.

"By the way," said Jim, "don't fret about Hairy's brag. The people think he conducted himself all right for a white man." Jim looked sideways at Tal. "You brought honor on yourself."

Tal felt glad at his friend's praise. Tal squatted to watch the dancing. The drums beat eternally. Tal thought drumbeats must fire the Indian soul. They made him feel queer, out of sorts with himself.

Soon Pine Leaf waved Tal into the center of the circle and called for quiet. The drumbeats faded to a pulse. Hairy put a big paw on Tal's shoulder and smiled down at him. Pine Leaf had two skin-wrapped bundles.

"Because our Long-Knife friends have brought honor and glory to our people," Pine Leaf called, "I wish to honor them in my own way."

She unfolded one skin and brought forth a book.

"Shakespeare," she said, "I give you Shakespeare." Hairy stepped out and took it from her hand.

"Tulloch says it is songs of the singer whose name you bear," Pine Leaf said.

Hairy held it up and roared, *"The Tragedies of Shakespeare.* The noblest lines in the English language speak from these pages."

He grabbed Pine Leaf's hand, bent low over it, and kissed it. She drew it back with an embarrassed smile, and a nervous titter was heard.

"Thank you, dear lady and comrade-at-arms."

Hairy withdrew, hugging Shakespeare to his huge chest.

"And I wish to honor Tal," she reached into the other bundle, "with this."

She drew out a long, long sash, like Tal saw at the fort that one day, and handed it to him.

He gawked at it. This one was entirely of sky-blue silk. The ends were decorated with elegant beadwork, and tasseled with braids of golden cloth.

"Wherever you go wearing this sash, you go with my blessing," said Pine Leaf.

Tal's knees gave, and he bumped down.

"As you went with the blessing of some other girl, my rival," she teased, "when you wore this handkerchief." She tugged at the silk blazon in her braid.

Tal started to rise, but Jim put a hand on Tal's shoulder, keeping him on his knees.

"One thing more," Antelope Jim called out, repeating himself in the Absaroka language. "James Pierson Beckwourth, hero of the mountain Crows, has a special gift for Tal as well. Hand me your lance," he said to Pine Leaf. She did and Jim lifted it high.

"I now shall knight you a new name, a badge of honor. Antelope Jim and his wives and Pine Leaf have chosen a name that stands for your style, your smoothness, your radiance.

"Therefore, by the power vested in me as war chief of the nation, which I got by popping the scalps off many Blackfoot heads, I hereby designate you Knight-Errant of the Absaroka people, and dub thee...Silk!"

He laid the lance blade on the left shoulder of the kneeling Tal, then the right.

"Arise, fair knight Silk, and go forth to mighty deeds!"

15

Thrice is he arm'd that hath his quarrel just
*   —Henry VI, Part 2, I.iii*

Tal had no idea where he was. The sun was up, for a long time—he could feel it on his face, and he was hot. He didn't intend to sit up yet, because he thought he'd be sick. Best let well enough alone. The sun on his eyelids was enough to see.

Seemed to be a lot he couldn't recall. Getting his sky-blue sash from Pine Leaf, that was there. Also getting the new name from Jim. Silk. "Silk," he whispered happily—and cringed. Sounded like hammer on rock in his head.

Let's see, after the name, he and Jim and Hairy raised several toasts to the newly christened knight. Then things got dim. He thought he recalled Pine Leaf trying to take him into a lodge to be with this girl who wanted him, and he felt like a fool and said no. No, no, no. He thought he remembered Hairy and Beckwourth having a rip-roaring wrestling match in front of a big audience—his recollection was that Jim had had the best of it, but he couldn't guess how. He could recall thinking he ought to pick a place to pass out. The rest was darkness.

He scooched and found out that whatever he was lying on was uncomfortable. He scooched again, harder—and sat halfway up in pain. Whoa! Dizzy! Falling back, he saw what he was lying on—poles.

Poles!

Jesusgawdamighty. He looked from side to side, turning his head ever so gingerly. He was ten feet off the ground, bedded down on lodgepoles propped through cottonwood limbs. No wonder his back and tail hurt.

He stared to sit up again, and discovered the earth starting to rotate on its axis. He flopped down quick.

Someone laughed. In a cavernous voice.

Tal lay back with his eyes closed and considered. He was on a scaffold, that's what this amounted to, a burying scaffold. Someone was funning him. *Somone,* meaning Hairy. Tal decided to kill *someone.*

Something was wrong with his arms too—they didn't work. Felt like they'd grown fast to his body.

Tal wasn't up to killing anyone just now anyway. He got dizzy just thinking about it.

He cracked one eye, then the other, and pointed them where his arms used to be.

He couldn't believe it.

"We wrapped you up like a Christmas present," Hairy intoned. "You be our sacrifice to Bacchus, god of the grape."

Tal was blinking. He'd been wrapped in a blanket and tied with his new sky-blue sash, making a giant bow. And it was pinning his arms snug.

"Wagh! You looked like you was gone under. You did so. Wagh!"

Tal decided this was too much. Time to get mad. He lifted his knees and got his hands beneath his thighs.

"Easy, hoss," called Hairy.

Tal lunged upward, meaning to sit.

The poles supporting him bent—that is, the flexible tips of two of the lodge poles flexed even more. Then they sprang back. Tal bounced up a little, and coming down smote the poles with his bottom.

They flexed deeper. They slid sideways on the branch. They skinnied off and headed for the ground. And shot the tied-up Tal right down the chute.

Tal threw up on the rough earth, sideways. He opened his eyes gingerly. He heaved once more, sort of testing, got nothing, and thought he could risk getting to his knees. At this eminence he swayed for a moment. Then he gently began to fumble around himself, he didn't know what for, maybe taking inventory. His skin was raging, like it had been rasped off. His head was gonging, like he'd been cold-cocked. He knew he was mashed here and there, like a stepped-on orange. He'd never felt so rotten in his life. He threw up again. *Someone* put a hand on his shoulder. Tal slapped it away and muttered, "Bandanna."

"This child be sorry...," Hairy started meekly.

"Bandanna!" Tal barked.

Cloth touched his hand, and he wiped his mouth and nose and eyes with it. He opened his eyes and saw red—everything awash in watery scarlet. He felt of his right eyebrow, and found it gashed and bleeding into the eye. When he wiped the eye, he could see. Sort of. At least see *someone* squatting there before him with a hangdog expression. Tal just looked.

"It was a joke we done, Jim and me," Hairy started whining. Tal felt so malicious he let the fool go on. "We made for it to be funny, on account of you was so out, to make a corpse o'ye, and..."

Tal was getting steady on his knees. As soon as he was steady enough, he was going to squash someone's big snout with his knuckles.

"You surely did look funny, too," Hairy babbled on, "a-tied up like for Christmas and fancied with a bow. This child be rightly sorry about your sash, Tal, I mean Silk, truly he be."

The sash. Tal took hold of himself. He grasped the ends of the big bow and awkwardly tugged until they untied and fell away from his arms. He unlooped them from around himself, and let the blanket drop, carefully maintaining his balance propped on his knees.

He inspected the sash.

It had grass stains, and dirt stains, on the beautiful sky blue.

And it was snagged and ripped where a limb had caught it and the earth had roughed it.

It was ruined. The sash Pine Leaf gave him was ruined.

Hairy had ruined it.

Tal lowered his head and took a deep breath. A broken tip of pole, long as a boy, was within reach. Without effort at concealment Tal reached for it, cocked it well back, and clubbed Hairy on top of the head.

The giant looked like he was going to cry. But seeing the look on Tal's face, he humphed to his feet, fussed for an instant, and took off running.

Tal was on his tail. He whapped the pole down on Hairy's shoulder.

Hairy dodged around a sagebrush. Tal followed, his stomach only a little whoop-de-doo on the curve. He could gain on the straightaways.

Hairy rumbled to the edge of a little dry wash, leaped in, and tried to scramble up the other side.

Tal caught him. The giant was clawing haplessly at the crumbly earth.

Tal laid it to him on the back. Hairy pretended not to notice. Tal whacked him on the head, and brought blood from the scalp.

Tal raised the pole overhead again, and started to lose his balance backward. Hairy, tears on his cheeks, put out a big hand, pushed Tal to the ground, and ran off down the wash, sending back a pathetic wail.

"Go find yourself another sucker for a partner," Tal screamed after him.

"You through?"

Antelope Jim was squatting on the bank, looking down at Tal, plopped in mid-wash.

"Yeah," said Tal bitterly, "I'm through with him."

Jim let this set.

"Through for good," Tal said, getting to his feet. "Partner like that—get me killed, or mocked, or run out of the country."

Jim stuck a hand down and helped Tal up the side of the wash.

"Man's gotta be a jackass to buddy up to that."

Jim said nothing, and handed Tal a canteen. When Tal had swigged deep, they started toward Jim's lodge. Tal saw Jim was carrying the sash, which Tal had left in the dirt. Well, to heck with the sash—it was all spoilt now.

Tal didn't have much to say over coffee. "Hangover cure," Jim muttered. Jim's wives served Tal in their one metal cup, which was a gesture of consideration for a guest. Only Little Wife spoke to him, and she carefully prefaced each sentence with his new name, Silk. The three women sat or kneeled at the back of the tipi while the men ate. Mad as he was, Tal couldn't help noticing that something was different. The women treated him like a warrior, not like a kid.

Well, I am a darn warrior, he thought to himself. Got the horse—well, a horse—and the scalps. Well,

Hairy got the scalps. Tal was half confused and half mad.

Jim started in easy. "You two got some bond, you know."

Silk just looked at him, harsh.

"You saved his life from the griz."

"Now I'm real thankful for that," said Silk sarcastically.

"And he saved yourn from the Cheyenne."

Silk snorted.

"He buddies you."

Silk slammed the metal cup onto the ground. Coffee splattered—Silk was glad it missed the hides, but made no move to pick up the cup. He crawled toward the door flap.

Jim folded up the sash and handed it to Little Wife. He spoke to her in the Crow language, too rapidly for Silk to pick up a word from outside. Then he joined Silk in the autumn morning.

It was cool, sunny, and promising. For a moment they stood there gazing around, ill at ease.

"Silk," Jim started in, "it's an open winter so far. Ought to be fair enough to travel for a spell yet. What say we go for a walk? I got something in mind."

Tal fidgeted and thumbed his belt downwards and nodded. "Don't care what we do," he allowed, "so long as it's far from Hairy."

So they got to packing, with Pine Leaf's help, and left without even telling Hairy goodbye.

16

all the good gifts of nature
—Twelfth Night, I.iii

Bu Antelope Jim evidently didn't care to say what something he had in mind. That after-noon and night and all the next day he had nothing to say. Trudged up South Fork with his eyes sharp on the countryside and his mouth shut. His legs cranked, and he sometimes raised one hand to shade his eyes against the glare. But no words.

Which was fine with Tal. Or Silk, as he tried to think of himself. Silk was trailing, letting his feet fol-low one another mechanically across the thin layer of snow, dwelling in his mind on his father once more. His father that had run off and left him. He was mad at his dad—he let himself grumble and grouse and study on looks of indifference in case he ever saw David Dylan Jones again.

Silk did not often let himself ponder the Reverend Mr. Jones, first a preacher of sermons and singer of praise, then improbably a fur trapper. This day Silk mulled on the son of a buck moodily. Several times he caught himself humming his dad's favorite hymn tunes, and bit his tongue.

They bivouaced with just a squaw fire, ate cold pemmican for dinner, and munched breakfast pemmican on the trail. On up South Fork they walked, moving easily because of so little snow. Silk wondered where they were headed, and why they went on foot instead of horseback, and whether their possible sacks provided enough to live on. But Jim was still silent, so Silk went back to mulling on mind pictures of his dad.

When they started into high country, the weather changed and so did Silk's mood. The wind took the half-cloudy, half-gray skies away, and the air got colder. Silk was warmer walking in the sun, but more chill in his blankets at night.

Near the big divide the vistas got bigger—Silk could study huge sweeps of the Yellowstone Mountains, running north and south. He could gaze across the hundred-mile-wide valley of the Big Horn River to the Big Horn Mountains in the east, high, remote, and glistening. Beyond the divide the country shut off the far horizons, cupped them in forested hills and rolling parks, like giant hands of the Creator. It was grand.

The meadows, only ankle-deep in snow, were almost innocent of tracks—the elk and deer had gone to lower ground to winter. The air was so crisp and clear you could have picked out moose a mile off, and told bull from cow at half a mile. The country was pristine, Silk said to himself. *Pristine* was one of his father's favorite words, used to describe the Garden of Eden God meant for man.

Silk noted the country in his head for mapping in his journal at night. He would leave a space for where they were going, and why, when he found out.

Jim's mood changed too. He was still all eyes, but he didn't look so wary now. Sometimes Silk caught Jim studying Silk's face, for what reason he couldn't figure.

On the fourth day they walked into a place—*the* place, Silk knew immediately.

An open meadow meandered in all directions, humping gently here, reaching out there, nestling against evergreen forests on three sides. At the top, the narrow end, stood several dozen elk, grazing tranquilly. And behind the elk, their secret—steam roiling up.

Water there. Boiling, evidently. Sulphuric, his nose told him. It's warm there, and the grass is bared, he thought.

Silk noticed Jim half-turned to look at him, smiling a little.

Near the steaming water, dead trees fingered black branches against the royal-blue sky. The lower branches were covered with rime ice and sparkled in the noon sun. Further back, pine branches hung heavy with snow that melted into long icicles.

An enchanted place, truly. Silk knew instantly that he would always remember this meadow, always treasure in his mind this first moment of seeing it. He felt magic-struck, like a child looking at illustrations of fairy stories in costly books. But this was better, for it was a grown man's fantasy, not a child's. And it was here. He could touch it. He intended to.

He looked his thanks at Jim for the gift of this place.

They walked beyond the elk, who seemed not to notice them—the tawny grass was easy to get at—and dropped their possible sacks upwind of the steam. The air was warmer here. Without a word Jim unloaded, stripped naked, walked to the water's edge, and disappeared into the mist.

Silk slipped his clothes off and hurried to the edge of the pool. He felt dicey, like breaking out in giggles and goose bumps at once. "Down here, hoss, "Jim called, "unless you're wanting to parboil yourself."

Silk stuck in a toe to test, and jerked it right back out.

"Here where the hot mixes with cold," Jim said.

His feet felt funny on the cold grass and rock. The water turned out to be just right.

Jim lolled back, eyes closed, let his head sink under water, then sat up and spouted like a whale. He gave Silk a snow-blinding smile.

Late that afternoon. The winter sun sinking low. Dollops of creamy light and violet shadow on the meadow snow.

They were luxuriating beyond luxurious. After half a day of lying in and getting hot, then lying out and getting chilled, they were back in the hot pools, soaking up the warmth. It seemed indecent to Silk to pamper the body in this way. He loved it.

He pampered the spirit as well. Played his love flute. Sat on the side and dangled his feet and tried out tunes on the thing. Even made some up for it. The flute wasn't well in tune with itself, and seemed unpredictable in some ways, but he could make music with it. Could get two octaves by overblowing. Even figured out how to play one of his dad's favorite traditional tunes, "Greensleeves," which he dedicated not to Pine Leaf but to the flute-maker, Ginny:

Alas, my love, you do me wrong
To cast me off discourteously,
for I have loved thee so long,
Delighting in thy company.

He refused to think of Pine Leaf and the humiliation of giving her the wrong horse. The only burrs under his saddle, little ones, were wondering if this place was all the something Jim had in mind, and a little tug of hunger.

Suddenly Jim stood up in knee-deep water, his big, muscled body gleaming wet. "Heap big hunter make meat," he pronounced self-mockingly.

He stepped onto the bank, picked up his wide leather belt, and fastened it around his bare waist. His hunting knife hung in its sheath in back, pointing between his buttocks. When Jim turned, Silk saw a scar on his thigh for the first time, a narrow, straight scar that went horizontally from thigh into the top of his crotch hair.

Jim saw him looking. "Now when I tell ye not to knife-fight Frenchies, you'll believe old Jim, huh."

"You mess with his woman?" Silk was conscious of sounding grown up.

"Naw, he was trying to gut me, not geld me. And he missed. He'd learn to keep that knife sharp, it wouldn't even show."

Jim touched his toes a couple of times. "You watch if this American ain't fiercer'n any Frenchman."

Jim started striding fast toward some elk fifty yards away.

Silk climbed out to watch, throwing a blanket around his shoulders.

As Jim got closer, the cows and calves began to lift their heads and drift off. One cow looked around to both sides, looked back at Jim, pawed nervously.

Jim bolted for the calf.

The little fellow made a bleat and headed higgledy-pig-gledly for the hillside, and the snow.

Jim burst after it. Silk had never seen a human creature run so fast, much less a naked human creature.

The cow sashayed after, uncertain.

Near the hill the calf cut right.

Jim darted across the angle.

The calf dived toward the hill, and was in snow to its shoulders.

Jim plunged after.

The cow galloped at Jim.

Just then Jim went down—scooted and buried himself.

The cow, almost there, slid and slithered and ran right over Jim.

A black man-creature raised up frosted.

The calf floundered toward its mother and bumped Jim from behind. He went down again.

For a moment the churning of bodies and snow. Then the cow and calf came lumbering out of the drift.

But where was Jim? The cow was hippety-hopping strangely.

A black arm flashed in the sun behind the cow's rump. The cow jerked.

Jim was on his knees grabbing for the other leg. His knife glinted. The cow sank onto its hindquarters.

The calf ran off, slipped in the snow, slid on its side, got up, and loped toward the other cows and calves.

Silk grabbed his clothes and Jim's and walked over. Sure enough, the cow was hamstrung.

Jim was laughing. Cackling so hard he couldn't stop. His black head was matted with snow, hair and beard alike. He was sitting in the snow, his warm butt melting him deeper.

Next to him was manure. On his chest and arm was manure. All over him was manure, where he'd been dragged through it. Jim started scraping it off with snow.

Finally Jim looked at Silk and giggled some more. Silk tossed him his pants.

"A man hunts like that, his hangy-downs could get chilled," Silk commented.

Jim cupped his a moment, squinched his nose, and said, "Feelin' fine."

Jim rose in the snow and beat his naked breast with his fists and howled a war cry. "This child done out-fierced the be-e-asts!"

Silk gave Jim a wry look and started slitting for the tenderloins.

17

Youth's a stuff will not endure

—Twelfth Night, II.iii

The next morning Jim was gone.

Silk woke up late—no Jim, no fire, no sign.

They'd stayed up half the night, gorging themselves on the elk and trading stories. Silk had slept in, but not Jim. Well, maybe he was gone after the something he had in mind.

Silk made a squaw fire, started a little meat roasting, and built a rack of limbs high over the fire. He spent the morning cutting the half-frozen elk into strips and spreading them on the rack.

At noon Jim came striding into camp empty-handed. He took in the drying set-up and nodded back toward the direction he'd come and said, "Let's go for a walk."

All right.

Jim had nothing more to say on the trail. They followed the hot-spring creek upstream into the woods and up a little canyon. In a couple of miles they came to a spectacular sight, a frozen waterfall. It was a narrow one, a vertical chute between rock walls. Jim sat down, still solemn-looking. Silk clambered down and touched the ice.

It was incredible. You could see the water, all its little jumpings and turnings and even sprayings. Yet it was still. As if some god had pointed a finger and caught it there in its playfulness and stopped it dead, putting a halt to time. Since then snow had fallen lightly onto the ice, gracing it gently as lace.

Silk looked up at Jim with a delighted smile, thanking him for the gift of the waterfall. But the black man returned Silk's look gravely and motioned him over.

Jim didn't speak but went on up the trail a few yards, Silk following. Jim turned off into a little glade and stopped at a big dead tree surrounded by boulders.

He climbed up the boulders and touched the tree with his finger.

Silk saw that the blazed mark made a Cross and that something was tacked to it. He came up the boulders and…

Silk reached out and put his hands on the piece of ribbon and then leaned his forehead on it and then his cheek. Silk hugged the tree. Jim saw tears on his face.

"Your dad's?" Jim said quietly.

Silk nodded and hugger harder. Sobs came now.

"Was afraid so."

Jim squatted on the boulder and got out his pipe and lit it. Eyes front, paying Silk no heed. His ears told him of sobs, and then sniffling. Jim sent smoke into the sky.

Finally he heard Silk working at the horseshoe nails that held the piece of ribbon on the tree. The lad sat next to Jim. On his open hand was a simple Cross made of two strips of scarlet ribbon, dirtied and torn. The initials D D J were stitched in gold thread down the center strip.

"Where is he?"

"Somewhere close. Under big rocks and not marked. Else Injuns or critters..."

Finally Silk asked, "How'd you know?"

"Heard tell. Jedediah Smith read verses over him, and the boys remembered that and spoke of it. Recalled the coon was said to be a preacher man, and thought it might be your dad. Had to hunt for a sign——Jedediah allus left one."

"How'd it happen?"

"Tale is he was playing on the rocks around the falls, slipped on the wet, smacked his head. Bad luck."

"Dad wasn't much for playing," Silk said.

Jim cast an eye upon him. "Maybe that's what he journeyed to the Shining Mountains for."

Silk stared sightless across the glade. "I journeyed to the Shining Mountains to find him."

Jim nodded. "I know."

How do you get used to the idea, Jim wondered, that you're never going to get something you want that bad? Silk was quiet a while, fingering the ribbon Cross. "Dad used this to mark his place in the Scripture," he said.

Jim nodded and puffed on his pipe. You don't get used to it, he supposed—you just hurt.

After a long time Silk stood up and walked off a little and looked long at the tree and the blazed Cross and Jim below it, and then at the waterfall where David Dylan Jones had died. He walked down and put his hand on the ice. It was hard, and cold, cold, cold.

Silk took one deep breath, and let it out lingeringly. "Thank you," he said to Jim with dignity, and headed down the trail.

What was there to do but head down the trail?

18

If the rascal have not given me medicines to make me love him, I'll be hanged
—*Henry IV, Part 1, II.ii*

Jim had Silk just right. If he'd been standing, he'd have been weaving. When he wasn't mumbling about enchantments, quarrels, battles, and other impossible follies, he was spilling his guts to Jim and Pine Leaf. Pine Leaf didn't understand, and Jim thought it was about half funny, but that didn't matter. It was Silk who needed to understand.

They were sitting there by the river while the early winter twilight deepened.

"Rescue fair damsels, defend the good, fight for the right, and stuff like that," Jim agreed. "Like your daddy taught you."

Silk looked to see if he was being mocked, but he wasn't. "Yeah," he agreed, "stuff like that." He raised a salute to the rising moon. "Knight errantry!" he called.

"But not too damn errant." Jim made it sound like a-a-a-runt.

They bobbed their heads in agreement, and Jim handed Silk the jug again. Silk had a little trouble balancing it while he got his swig.

"Now," Jim said with quiet emphasis to Pine Leaf. She got up and walked off.

Jim had built the small sweat hut this afternoon and got Pine Leaf to be the helper, the one who handed in the heated rocks with a stick. He'd taken Silk through all four rounds, the round of four cups of water tossed onto the rocks, the round of seven cups, the round of ten, and the round of uncounted cups, meaning uncounted wishes. The steam had gotten to be some—Jim himself had about passed out from the heat.

But the dip in the freezing river had jolted them back to their senses half way, and the jug held them only half way while Jim waited for the perfect moment.

Silk had started by telling stories of Don Quixote, that wondrous knight of old who cared not a fig for odds. Then he told about his dad, and even his mom, and spun a good story about the family fishing together on the Mississippi. He'd talked about feeling second-class in St. Louis, where the folks who counted spoke French and rode in carriages. He'd talked about hating his dad for being a wretched father, and loving him for the Welsh poesy that sang in his blood.

When Jim asked what good that Welsh poesy would do Daddy's son, Silk had answered in a silly way, but meaning it, that it gave him the temperament of a knight errant: "My fantasy is filled with those things that I have read," Silk quoted giddily again, and Jim didn't hear the rest.

Sometimes you had to get 'em drunk, or such-like.

Silk turned half-serious. "Jim," he asked levelly, "I want you to go with me. Partner me." Silk's cast-down eyes said the request was all serious, but he didn't want to face it square. "We'll have a hundred barrels of fun."

"You mistake me for what's his name…Pancho?"

"No, you ain't a Sancho Panza, I know that." Silk grasped Jim by the shoulder, comrade-like. "Think of all the stuff we could do."

"Hoss," said Jim seriously, "my life is here with the Crow people. My kids is here." Silk wasn't meeting his eyes. "I got to stay at least until I marry up with Pine Leaf, and then a while to enjoy diddling her."

"Yeah, I know," Silk said, sorry for himself.

"You got to go along with somebody else."

Just then Pine Leaf got back, Hairy hanging behind her. Jim didn't blame Hairy, really, for sulking. Since Jim and Silk got back from the grave of Silk's dad yesterday, Silk had avoided Hairy completely, mostly sticking to Jim's lodge.

"Set," Jim ordered Hairy, tapping the ground.

"I won't…" Silk started.

"Shut your mouth," Jim told Silk. "Set," he told Hairy, tapping the ground.

The big man lowered his butt to the earth, looking shamefaced. Jim handed Hairy the jug, and Hairy swigged. Jim motioned for him to swig again, and he did.

"Tell your partner what a louse he is," Jim ordered Silk.

Silk got up, unsteadily, to go. Jim jerked him down by the hand.

"Tell him," Jim repeated.

Silk glared back at Jim as long as he could.

"All right," Silk croaked. "You dummy! You idiot!" Jim made Hairy drink while Silk hollered. "You've likely got half the Cheyenne nation on our tails come spring."

Hairy looked at Silk mournfully.

"It's so, ain't it?" Silk insisted. Hairy made a face. "Say it's so, darn you!" Silk bellered.

"It's gospel," murmured Hairy, hurt. When he nodded, the curls of the chestnut wig bobbed.

"You stalked a bear, only it was stalking you. Woulda ate you except for me." Silk waited, glowering.

"It's God's truth," said Hairy, sounding like he'd cry if a man could cry. Pine Leaf handed him the jug and he imbibed once more.

Silk was on his feet now, weaving and gesturing. "And you built a huge fire like a kid and set the grass on fire. Lucky it didn't spook the horses."

"Likely so," said Hairy. He was beginning to take it amiss now.

"You're a God—goshdarned fake and cheat and... you ruint my sash and..."

Jim pushed Silk into Hairy. They got tangled up and rolled on the ground and Silk came up with his fists ready.

"Hit him," said Jim to Silk.

Silk hesitated.

"Hit him or I'll hit you."

Silk jabbed Hairy in the mouth.

"Fight back," snapped Jim at Hairy. "Now."

Hairy shook his huge head. "He's muh partner."

Pine Leaf grabbed Hairy's arms. Jim slapped Hairy in the face flat-handed. It stung, and it stunned, Jim could see.

"Fight him or fight us all three. Now." Jim slapped him again.

Silk punched Hairy in his big gut.

Jim shoved Hairy into Silk. They went down and rolled around and came up scrapping. Hairy rose bald-headed.

Pine Leaf covered a giggle with her hand.

It was a ridiculous fight, the gnat and the elephant. Silk would prance around out of reach, then dart in and hit Hairy. The blows looked puny. Hairy slugged back at Silk, but slowly, without rage.

Silk was getting madder, though, and frustrated. Finally he rushed Hairy and tried to strangle him. So Hairy couldn't avoid getting his gigantic arms around Silk. Then the elephant ran the gnat backward into a tree.

Boy and man lay there stunned. Silk was trying to find some air somewhere in the world. Hairy was trying to figure out what he'd done.

Suddenly Silk came out with his skinning knife and jumped for Hairy. Pine Leaf tripped him, and Jim kicked the knife away.

"Keep it clean, boys," warned Jim. Hairy's eyes were on Silk's empty knife hand, and the whites were showing. "Hit but don't grab," Jim warned.

It was a hellacious battle, Jim thought, considering. Silk was to-hell-and-gone mad now, and Hairy had decided morosely that he'd like to teach the little sumbitch who's who.

Hairy kept shuffling in, pumping those hammer hands out front heavy but slow. Silk would dart under or around and lick Hairy a good one. Hairy sent him sprawling with swipes a couple of times, but Silk got his fair share in, and maybeso more. Jim had a willow limb to trip one of them with, but he didn't need it.

Silk would have won if he could have hurt Hairy, but it was like whipping a bear with a switch.

"They are mad to kill," Pine Leaf said softly to Jim. Meaning mad enough to kill. Yeah, it would have helped if they'd been able to hurt each other more. Jim didn't *think* either would get hurt. Not serious, anyway. He treated himself to a swallow.

"A glug of the jug," Jim murmured, feeling pleasantly high.

Just then Silk charged and Hairy caught his arm and used his momentum to fling him at a cottonwood. Silk hit it flat on his back, whumphed like he'd fallen off a roof, and slid to the ground.

Jim started to yell at Hairy for grabbing, but it was too late. The big man was rared up to go. Jim moved fast.

Hairy leapt, meaning to land on Silk, just as Jim kicked him.

Hairy went sprawling across the hard ground. Quick, he recovered and crawled toward the downed Silk.

And burst into tears.

He picked Silk up. Cradled him. "My Corde-e-elia!" he wailed.

Silk was pretending to be out, watching Hairy through half-closed eyes for the main chance.

Hairy set Silk down on the cold earth, hovered over him. He orated,

Why should a dog, a horse, a rat, have life,
And thou no breath at all?

Silk smothered a chuckle. Jim smirked. They looked at each other with mirth in their eyes.

In the silence Pine Leaf laughed out loud. Jim lost control and ho-hoed because she didn't know what was funny.

Silk guffawed. He rolled over and pounded his knees. He rested his head on the ground and shook with joy.

Tears began to roll down Hairy's face. He wept silently, the great chest trembling a little.

Seeing the tears, Jim called "Whoo-e-ee!" He had another tipple.

Silk looked up at Hairy's grief-stricken face and grabbed his partner by the shoulders.

Hairy lifted his profile to the lavender evening sky, eyes still closed, nose noble as a dung heap.

Jim grabbed both of them into a bearhug, a three-man squeeze.

They toppled over.

Prone, Jim managed another swig. He handed the bottle to Silk, who pulled at it avidly. Hairy took a tot. Pine Leaf handed him the wig, and he covered his naked head and wispy scalplock.

Sprawled all over each other, they had one more round.

Jim pushed himself upright. He lifted one arm to the sky, the jug dangling from a finger. "Here's to friends," he announced, "the friendship of men who've saved each others' tails."

Hairy struggled to his feet, raised the jug to the moon.

The friends thou hast,

quoth Polonius to his son,

Grapple them to thy soul with hoops of steel.

Jim motioned Pine Leaf over. "Get it for him," he said.

She was back in just one more round of the jug. She held something out in the moonlight. "Little Wife fixed it," Pine Leaf said gently.

The sash.

Silk felt suddenly sober. He took it and examined the damaged places. It had been cleaned somehow. The tear was covered by…by a long strip of soft, white doeskin decorated with some beadwork. Silk held it up to the moonlight. He couldn't make out the pattern of the beadwork.

"Silk and Shakespeare, it says," Jim murmured from behind. "The names Silk and Shakespeare bind the sash together."

19

amaze, indeed,
The very faculties of eyes and ears
—Hamlet, II.ii

On the first day of spring—or it seemed such—a Frenchy arrived at the village with a message from Mr. Tulloch, the trader down to the fort. Tulloch wanted to see Silk and Hairy —*beaucoup importe,* said the Frenchy.

"Errand," said Jim. "Spot of cash money."

"An errand for knights errant," intoned Hairy.

They talked it over. Winter with the Crows had been tedious. For a while Silk liked listening to the stories of old times, stories that were more like Bible stories, but it got wearisome. The moon of frost in the tipi put an end to hunting and riding and near everything but sitting around. That moon gave way to three new moons and there was nothing to do but visit folks' lodges and listen to old people tell more stories. Silk even preferred listening to Hairy read from his one-volume Shakespeare tragedies.

And cash money. Jim said the Crows wouldn't stir from the spot for a month—not until the ponies got stronger. Why not have an adventure in the meantime? A paying adventure? They rode to Fort Cass with the Frenchy.

Tulloch's proposition was simple. He'd heard about the boys' whupping the Cheyennes. Even heard it was a trifle excessive. Seemed like a good idea for them to clear out of the country for a while.

So Tulloch had a suggestion, spoken in his ironical manner. Maybe they'd like to carry letters over to Fort Union, down at the mouth of the Yellowstone. Not far— ten sleeps each way. He'd give them a hundred dollars.

Tulloch went back to making marks in whatever ledger he was working in, like he didn't care.

Silk and Hairy talked it over outside.

"He just wants no trouble around the fort," Hairy protested.

"Good idea," Silk answered.

"Hoss, they couldn't tell me without my crazy paint," Hairy said craftily.

"The woods is full of three-hundred-pound giants," mocked Silk.

"They think I'm dee-vine," Hairy grinned.

"They heard the rumor you're mortal," replied Silk.

Hairy pulled at his chin. "Let's ask for more money," he suggested.

"That darn Tulloch would like any excuse to back out," said Silk, leading the way back in.

"Go the long way around," advised Tulloch. He kept fussing with his books. "Everybody's heard by now. Most particular the Cheyennes."

Silk cocked an eye at Hairy. "Stealing a horse on the sly and less conspicuous might help."

"That," Hairy said cheerfully, "ain't this child's style."

Tulloch grunted.

Silk asked after his daughter Ginny—wanted to compliment her on the flute, he said. Tulloch looked mean at Silk and mumbled something about Ginny being out of the fort.

It was an easy trip.

The long way was over the divide onto the Musselshell River and down it. They could have travelled down the Yellowstone to its mouth, where Fort Union was—they could even have gone by canoe, or bullboat—but the Cheyennes were along the Yellowstone somewhere, or close by.

Heading north on strong horses borrowed from Tulloch, they struck the Musselshell where it makes its big bend to the north and followed along it almost to Big Muddy, the Missouri.

"This being Bug Boy land," as Hairy put it, Blackfoot country, they were light and quick, ate only dried food, made only squaw fires. Yet everything was so pleasant, the days so balmy, the new grass coming on strong, that it seemed an idyll.

They came into Fort Union the eighth day.

"Hoss," said Hairy, "this is some."

Where Fort Cass was a simple stockade, Fort Union was a sort of castle under the banner of John Jacob Astor, the clever New York financier, and Pierre Chouteau, the la-dee-da St. Louis aristocrat.

"Mr. McKenzie is out riding," said the clerk, who introduced himself as Mr. Hamilton, no first name. He made it sound, Silk thought, like any fool might fork a horse, but only a great man could go riding.

"You may leave the letters." Hamilton held out a bossy hand for them.

"Yes, sir," said Hairy, and gave them over.

"He will send for you tonight before dinner," the clerk informed them in cultivated British tones. "There will be food with the *engagés.*"

Well, at your service, *sir.* Silk wished he could break wind, just to show something.

Their room was tiny and had narrow beds. Imagine sleeping indoors, Silk thought, and all cramped like that.

They accepted the offer of a tour of the facilities. "Baronial," Hairy whispered to Silk, drawing the word out. The stockade extended two or three hundred feet in each direction, with walls twenty feet high and bastions in opposite corners. The house for the bourgeois and his wives—their escort made the plural distinct—was one-and-a-half stories high.

"She's even outfitted," said their guide, a Negro who spoke French-accented English, "with a cellar where Mr. McKenzie keeps wines and brandies that come all the way from France."

Hairy looked at the fellow with disgust. He always turned a little grape-colored when he got irritated.

"No, no, is true," said the *engage*. "We are here civilized. Did you know the steamboat comes here first time last summer? Is true."

Silk and Hairy looked at each other. Next the employees of Fort Union would be enjoying shrimp from New Orleans, or chippies from St. Louis.

"Brings many new things civilized. Wines and brandies, Mr. McKenzie's cigars…"

The black man gave them a glance of cunning. "Also what with to make a—how you call it —*still*, for the making of spirits. Is clever."

"Whooee!" said Hairy to Silk with a wink. Since booze was forbidden in Indian country, and the government occasionally tried to enforce the ban, McKenzie was taking the direct approach. In-dee-pendent.

The guide gave them a boyish smile, one that would have charmed the sphinx. "Mr. McKenzie is very proud for civilization here," he informed them.

Hairy withdrew into thought.

They had a powder magazine big enough to blow up the entire nation of Assiniboins, the local Indians, the tribe that supplied women for Mr. McKenzie. Shops for the gunsmith, tinsmith, and blacksmith. Huge fur press. Best of all, a room for dickering and trading, outfitted with plenty of store-bought goods from St. Louis. Here Hairy perked up and dickered with Mr. Hamilton at length and, despite outrageous prices, did buy two items—a dress and a skirt.

Mr. Hamilton's face gave no hint that the choices were unusual.

"A *dress* and a *skirt?*" snickered Silk outside.

"Wait and see, lad, this child's got an idee."

McKenzie was cordial, welcomed them heartily, inquired about the difficulty of their trip, and whether they'd sighted any Indians.

"Mr. Hamilton has already recorded the hundred dollars to your credit," he said lightly, "for any goods you like." He added that in the future, if they wished to work for American Fur again, they would be compensated more generously.

Silk wanted to ask for cash instead of credit, but Hairy silenced him with an imperious eyebrow.

McKenzie seemed about to dismiss them, then apparently got a sudden idea. "Would you like jobs? American Fur is looking for experienced trappers like yourselves. I can offer one thousand dollars a year."

Mr. Hamilton came in with written receipts for the hundred, and McKenzie handed them to Hairy, who gave them to Silk nonchalantly.

"Sir," Hairy began in his most cultivated British tones, "we would like to serve you, for treasure or for honor, but we seldom trap." Hamilton was staring at Hairy. "We merely seize the moment, as in bringing you these dispatches. Trappers errant, you might call us. But we could grace your evening, and that of your ladies, with another service." McKenzie was intrigued, or amused. "What is that?"

We would drown the stage with tears,
And cleave the general ear with heroic speech,
Make mad the guilty, and appall the free,
Confound the ignorant, and amaze, indeed,
The very faculties of eyes and ears.

Hairy had never spoken more sonorously, more musically, or louder. Silk thought he had a certain dignity, even majesty.

McKenzie traded glances of high hilarity with Hamilton. "An actor, a purveyor of the Bard in this wild and barren land!" exclaimed the head man. "We beg you, sirrah," McKenzie continued, "to 'amaze the faculties of our eyes and ears' after dinner. And to share a cordial with us after your performance."

Hairy fussed and fidgeted and looked about to speak.

"You may depend on our largesse," added McKenzie, smiling unctuously.

Having no idea what was up, Silk said to himself, we're in trouble. *I'm* in trouble.

20

naked, he was, for all the world, like a forked radish
—*Henry IV, Part 2, III.ii*

By curtain time (not that there was a curtain), Silk had nailed down McKenzie's "largesse" as fifty dollars, which was probably generous. And Silk was getting the entire fifty. It took at least that to get him to wear that cussed skirt.

Hairy was so avid to perform—"to tread the boards once more, lad"—he was glad to do it for nothing. Or for glory, which was either more or less than nothing, depending on your point of view.

The skirt, not being designed for Lady Macbeth but for a squaw, was a red calico affair, full and floor-length, tied around the waist. Hairy was tying Silk's sash into an immense bow in back. Silk wore a white blouse above it, and insisted on remaining flat-chested.

"Looks fine, lad, you being so willowy. The bow makes you downright pretty."

Silk wrinkled his nose at Hairy.

"It is the actor's pride, my boy" (he pronounced it "ahctoar" as usual) "to appear in many guises, to seem what he is not. Truly, his pride."

Silk didn't say that what bothered him most was feeling so naked, right up to his drawers, which was the last pair he had, and was holey. In fact, if his thing was placed just right, it dangled out one hole. Which felt extra airy.

Silk stood there in the dining room, which Hairy called the wings, looking through the crack in the door at the audience. He kept the skirt tight between his knees.

Seated in front were McKenzie and Hamilton, fancily decked out. On a sofa next to McKenzie were three Indian women dressed in gowns such as Silk had seldom seen, even in St. Louis, made with fine materials in gay colors. Silk supposed these were the wives or mistresses people spoke of—for sure they were beauties. To the rear were sitting several other men Silk didn't recognize. McKenzie and Hamilton had brandies and cigars and were talking quietly.

One of the squaws was holding a pair of opera glasses in her lap, for what reason Silk couldn't imagine, since it was only a drawing room. She kept studying the walls and such and giggling to her friends like a kid. Silk wrapped the skirt tighter around his legs.

Hairy was standing still, head in hands, like he was meditating or going over his lines once more. Silk felt sure of forgetting his own lines, however much

Hairy had drilled him all afternoon. Darn that *Tragedies of William Shakespeare.* Even fifty dollars wasn't enough. But Silk wasn't going to back out now. His partner was primed.

Silk's stomach sailed a little. Whoa! Whenever he touched his curly brown wig or rubbed his reddened lips together, he felt queasy. Better to back out than throw up. But Hairy said this was just stage fright, and turned to excitement with the first step onto the stage.

In his own get-up—Van Dyke beard, tights, doublet, overarched eyebrows, black-lined eyes, and white wig—Hairy looked the fool as well, a crazed, dangerous fool.

Hairy drew a ten-gallon breath, nodded for Silk to open the door, and strode mightily onto the stage.

He eyeballed the audience haughtily. Someone started to applaud, but Hairy's bald glance put a stop to that.

Honour pricks me on.

He said it confidentially, in a large whisper. He paused after that first word, like it was a coin he was inspecting.

Yea, but how if *honour* prick me off when I come on? how then?

He moved his huge bulk a couple of steps, limping heavily.

Can honour set-to a leg? No. Or an arm? No. Or take away the grief of a wound? No. Honour hath no skill at surgery, then? No.

Hairy turned to the audience, a great cat about to pounce.

What is *honour?* A *word.*

Silk thought Hairy was wonderful. It gave him the shivers.

What is that word, *honour?* Air.

Hairy held out an empty hand and contemplated its emptiness.

Now he suddenly bounded nimbly over the lines, water running downhill:

A trim reckoning! Who hath it? He that died o' Wednesday. Doth he feel it? No. Doth he hear it? No. It is insensible then? Yea, to the dead.

Hairy paused greedily, like the lion over the downed calf.

But will it not live with the living? No. Why? Detraction will not suffer it. *Therefore...*

Hairy reduced his voice to a happy squeak.

I'll none of it: honour is a mere scutcheon: and so ends my catechism.

He finished with a bow and a low-swept hand.

The applause was more than a dozen people could possibly make.

Silk was thrilled. He was hopping from foot to foot. He couldn't wait for his entrance. He wished he had a mirror to check his lip rouge—where, oh where was that silly stage fright now? Hairy stepped forward to address the audience. He was brimming over with himself now.

"Mr. McKenzie," he began, "ladies and gentlemen. Having submitted for your pleasure a few dance steps of that glorious rascal Falstaff, we give you a *pas de deux* by those master villains, Macbeth and his lady. A *pas de deux de la mort.*"

He reached out the door, took a tam o' shanter from Silk, and pulled it down onto his Falstaffian head.

Is this a dagger which I see before me,
The handle toward my hand? Come, let me clutch thee.

His voice was grander now, more terrible, a little tremulous.

I have thee not, and yet I see thee still.
Art thou not, fatal vision, sensible
To feeling as to sight? or art thou but
A dagger of the mind, a false creation
Proceeding from the heat-oppressed brain?

Hairy's hand groped for the knife that appeared only to Macbeth's fevered mind, grasping at thin air in search of substance.

At this moment a knife rose from the audience in a high and graceful arc. It turned once at the top of its flight, lazily, fell point downward, and stuck in the wood floor, quivering.

O! he's as tedious
As a tired horse, a railing wife.

It was Mr. Hamilton's plummy voice from the audience. "Try the real thing."

Hamilton sat back down, cackling at his own cleverness.

Oh, Lord, a heckler! Silk's stomach started floating again.

Hairy picked up the floor-stuck dagger and approached Hamilton menacingly.

"A devil haunts thee in the likeness of a fat old man," he said with an eerie smile.

Falstaff sweats to death,
answered Hamilton contemptuously,
And lards the green earth as he rolls along.
Hairy answered in thunder.
Away, you scullion! you rampallion! you fustilarian! I'll tickle your catastrophe!

On the word *catastrophe* Hairy placed the tip of the knife delicately between Mr. Hamilton's legs, firm against the crotch, and let go the handle. Hamilton grabbed it before the blade could go anywhere.

This amused McKenzie, who murmured, "Well done, well given back."

Silk breathed again. Hairy sneered and returned to the stage. He mused, stroking his Van Dyke.

I go and it is done; the bell invites me.
Hear it not, Duncan; for it is a knell
That summons thee to heaven or to hell.

And he rushed off the stage opposite Silk and immediately back on. He was holding high his own dagger, bloodied with vermilion.

Silk could see he was big with it now, he was going to be immense. His very strides were immense.

I have done the deed! Didst thou not hear a noise?

He paused. He waited. He looked around in agitation.

I have done the deed! Didst thou not hear a noise?

Hairy glared at Tal's entry door furiously.

"Wherefore, oh, wherefore art thou, Lady Macbeth?" crooned Hamilton.

Silk was late for his entrance!

"I have done the deed,"

cried Hairy for the third time.

Silk rushed toward Hairy, blotting the audience out of his mind.

The ladies tittered. McKenzie cackled.

The little dog laughed to see such sport,

said Hamilton.

Didst thou not hear a noise?

Hairy said once more.

Silk picked up his cue at last.

I heard the owl scream and the cricket cry

he said in a boy's voice, quaveringly.

Her voice was ever soft,
Gentle, and low, an excellent thing in woman,

quoth Hamilton.

"Cordelia," murmured McKenzie.

With an irritable glance at the audience, Hairy swept onward.

Methought I heard a voice cry, 'Sleep no more!
Macbeth doth murder sleep!'
What do you mean?

piped Silk.

Still it cried 'Sleep no more!' to all the house!

Hairy crooned. He began this next in a roar and finished in a whine.

Glamis hath murdered sleep, and therefore Cawdor
Shall sleep no more: Macbeth shall sleep no more!
Silk couldn't remember his line.

"Wish I could sleep," stage-whispered Hamilton.
What do you mean?
Silk repeated, desperate. He knelt down, maybe to apologize for forgetting the line—the kneeling was unrehearsed. His heart was fluttering wildly.

Hairy knelt before him, very close, the bloody dagger in one hand.
I'll go no more.
I am afraid to think what I have done;
Look on't again I dare not.
Hairy brought the dagger up and gazed on it, quavering.

He cued Silk from the upstage side of his mouth, "Take the dagger."

Silk's stomach did two somersaults, but he pressed on. He seized the blade, sprang to his feet, holding it boldly aloft, and cried,
Infirm of purpose!
Too late. He felt the tug around his waist and the cool on his legs and heard the chortling laughter and looked down to see himself bare to his drawers. His skirt was on the floor, pinned by Hairy's big knee.

His nethermost garment was his blue silk sash, which hung like a tail behind. Through the fatal hole in his drawers dangled his thing, a wilted flower.

The laughter was mounting.

Silk reached between his legs, grabbed the ends of his bow, and diapered himself.

The laughter was uproarious.

Hairy picked up the skirt, hoisted Silk in one arm, and ran off the stage brandishing the knife and crying,

For Harry, England, and St. George!

Tumultuous laughter and applause.

Hairy gripped Silk fiercely.

"Let me down, you idiot!" Silk howled.

Tidal waves of applause. Cheers.

Hairy draped the skirt over Silk's nether regions, whirled, and strode back onto the stage.

Silk thought he would pass out.

"All planned, lad, remember," Hairy muttered low. "Meant that way."

Cheers and whistles.

Hairy bowed low, his face grave, holding Silk like an armload of roses.

"Smile at the folks," Hairy murmured to Silk, face down. "Smile at the folks."

Silk turned his face into Hairy's Falstaffian belly.

21

thou art death's fool

—Measure for Measure, II.iv

"Uhn-uhn-uhn."
It was his own voice.

Somebody was tapping him.

Yellow Foot's face.

He rolled over and closed his eyes again.

The tapping came back and it was Yellow Foot's face, sweet and girlish.

Oh, yeah, the girls. He looked across the room and they were still there, lying next to Hairy under the blankets.

He remembered them, one girlish and delicate-looking and very naughty and the other tall and horse-faced. McKenzie had sent them to the room, with a quart of good awerdenty and his compliments a thousand times over.

They wanted to make the beast with two backs, as Hairy called it. At least they expected to.

Silk remembered what happened. He put them off and felt the fool.

He also remembered what he imagined happening. He dallied with the delicate one and didn't get mad until he found out that Hairy, and the ladies, expected to take turns. Silk fled to the bottle.

In another fantasy he enjoyed himself lustily with both of them in deliciously creative ways until he passed out. Hairy wasn't in this memory at all.

In his favorite memory he lay there naked and the girls stroked him with their cool hands.

Upshot: He was still a foolish virgin.

He turned his head. A-a-agh! The tippling part wasn't fantasy. A bodacious hangover.

Tap, tap.

Oh, yeah. Yellow Foot. What was Yellow Foot doing here? He turned and looked into Yellow Foot's gentle face.

Yup, Yellow Foot was here. The Indian motioned outside. Regretting his waking state, his headache, his very existence, Silk got up and followed Yellow Foot out.

Easing through the door, he looked down. Good. He had his pants on.

They slipped down to the river. "Hairy, he in trouble," Yellow Foot began.

"Yeah, with me," Silk said. But he couldn't think of any way to explain why that wasn't humiliating.

After a little Yellow Foot went on. "Cheyenne want him. Lots."

Silk pondered this. He nodded his head sagely several times. It figured. Well, they could go around

Cheyenne country on the way back to Fort Cass, just like they had gone getting here. They'd be pretty safe from the Cheyennes living with the Crows.

"Antelope Jim say this." Yellow Foot handed over a piece of paper. It was folded tight and said in block letters on the outside "SILK."

Silk—

Tulloch says Shians hot for Hairy, know where you are. Likely ambush way back. Be careful. McKenzie wants Shian trade bad—watch out, don't trust. Stay clear of Shians. It's Hairy they want, not you, so they got the story straight.

It was unsigned.

Silk folded the paper, then thought better of it, and set out to burn it.

Fiddling with flint and steel gave him time to think. His first thought was that McKenzie would sell out anybody, for the fun of it.

Silk looked at Yellow Foot. So Yellow Foot, he of the doe eyes, had made the trip from Fort Cass alone, in danger, to warn them. Must be 'cause he owed them one from the business of the wrong horse. They were sure square now.

He clasped Yellow Foot on the shoulder. "Thanks."

He pondered. Couldn't let Yellow Foot get any more mixed into it, or he'd be wolf bait too. Silk fished out his little journal, tore out a page, and scribbled on it. "Give Antelope Jim this message, please," he said.

The words written were: "Thousand thanks to you and Yellow Foot. Gave him this paper for you so he'd get clear."

Yellow Foot nodded and smiled and got up. Self-consciously, he stuck out his hand for Silk to shake. It was as limp a handshake as Silk had ever felt, but a winning smile came with it.

Then Yellow Foot moved off toward a grove of cotton-woods. Probably had his horse hid there. That was the way of him—do the necessary and move on.

Silk liked him.

Now he needed a scheme. A heck of a scheme.

"Damn, this…child…gone…*truly* die," Hairy wheezed.

He was up to his neck, naked in the Missouri. Ice was still floating in the river.

Darn right he was cold—that was the idea—Hairy should be clammy to the touch, in case anyone wanted to check. Silk smiled and leaned out and pushed him under again. Hairy'd feel cold as death, all right.

It had been Hairy's idea, naturally. At first Silk said he wasn't having any more of Hairy's strokes of thespian genius. Then he pondered how satisfying it would be to fool the imperious McKenzie and his snob henchman Hamilton…

"Hoss," Hairy said while they were doing the make-up, "it will be my most magnificent performance. Many actors have died onstage," he gloated, "but nary a one has played a corpse with his life in the balance!"

He was working on the brown wig, feathering vermilion into the hairs lightly. Behind the ear was a dark hole, so red it was nearly black, about .50 caliber size, with red dripping from it. Silk had to admit it looked very convincing.

"Remember, lad, *they* don't know it's a wig."

Hairy cut a scalping hole at the top center of the wig and dabbed red all around it. He wailed a little about ruining the wig—it couldn't be replaced. Well, maybe it could be patched. He saved the plug.

Then he watched carefully with his hand mirrors while Silk made a big red blotch on top of his bald head to represent where the scalp was taken. It took a lot of work, and used up about all their vermilion.

Finally, Hairy said, "Lad, it's a masterwork." Silk thought it was pretty good himself. He even got squeamish about touching it, there toward the end.

Hairy rubbed gray make-up into his face, but Silk didn't let him overdo it—"You'll look pallid from the river," Silk pointed out.

A bullet hole in the head. A bloody patch where scalp was missing. Pallor. Clamminess.

Ought to work.

At last Hairy's protests got worrisomely feeble, and Silk helped him out of the water. The poor fellow was blue and the touch of him gave Silk the chills. It also gave him a thrill of revenge.

They made tracks for the fort, Hairy draped across the saddle.

"I'll be wanting a box, Mr. Hamilton." He tied Hairy's horse.

"My boy…"

"A box." Silk bit the words off hard. "For a wooden overcoat."

The *engagés* were clustering about, not too close, crossing themselves. A breed child reached out and touched Hairy's hand, which dangled nearly to the ground. The kid jerked his hand away.

"We have no mill here," Hamilton stammered, "I…"

For a snob, Hamilton sure flustered easy in the presence of something real, like death.

"Mr. Hamilton, my friend is dead. I mean to do right by him. I want a box, and a couple of men to dig a grave. You can scrape up the boards. Hairy's credit will cover it."

"I suppose…"

McKenzie came up, a hard look on his face. He walked around the horse, squatted, looked at Hairy's head. Hairy's eyes were shut, his mouth was gaping open. He was giving it everything.

"Seven foot long, Mr. Hamilton, remember. Hairy was six and a half feet tall."

McKenzie touched Hairy's hand, grimaced, and stood up. Hand must have been nice and clammy, Silk thought, while pretending not to notice.

"Who did this?" McKenzie demanded.

"Darned if I know."

Hairy had coached him to be short with his answers, and prickly.

"How did it happen? We don't let killings of white men go unpunished."

"We were setting traps. Hairy got too darn far away. I come running at the shot, but you see I was too late."

"Who did it?"

"How in heck would I know?" This way of talking to Baron McKenzie was fun.

"Who would want to do it?"

Silk shrugged. "All it takes in this country is being a white man."

McKenzie spoke softly to Hamilton, too softly for Silk to hear.

Silk wondered if the baron knew about the Cheyenne troubles. Probably send word of his disapproval to Leg-in-the-Water, along with a list of the latest prices.

Silk borrowed a shovel and led Hairy's horse, bearing the immense corpse, off to the little burial plot.

While Silk dug—Hairy had to lie still, in case someone looked—Hairy speculated on staying in the coffin to hear Silk's funeral sermon. "How many men get to hear themselves eulogized, lad? You'll do it grand—it's in your blood."

But he was scared of having the lid closed dark down on him, being lowered into the grave, and having to hear the shovelfuls of dirt thud down inches above his eyes.

Sprawled out there playing a corpse, while Silk did the digging work, Hairy put his theatrical imagination to work on how it would feel. He whacked his belly flat-handed to get the sound of dirt thumping on the lid.

"Be still," Silk barked.

Hairy looked at him sheepishly.

Silk threw a spadeful of dirt onto Hairy's belly. "You wanna know how it would feel? "Silk teased. "Here." He heaved a shovelful onto Hairy's neck.

Forbidden to move enough to be seen, Hairy turned his head sideways and made a dead face, tongue hanging out.

Silk couldn't help laughing.

Silk had tried to think of a way to rule this burial out, if he could just figure how to get Hairy gone and the coffin filled with rocks without risk of being seen. It was tricky. Then the skirt fiasco came to mind again, and he suddenly thought how Hairy deserved to be buried alive.

He told Hamilton the funeral would be at sunset, which was the only way it could be timed. He'd have to bury Hairy and then get him out before he suffocated, or died of fright or superstition.

Hamilton said the *engagés* loved a funeral. Too bad they didn't have a priest, Hamilton allowed.

No need for any priest, brother Hamilton, Silk said to himself. This child didn't listen to David Dylan Jones from the front pew all those years for nothing. This child shall do it grand. And nasty.

22

then grace us in the disgrace of death
—Love's Labours Lost, I.i

A round the fresh grave the fort crew was gathered not only the common herd of Frenchies, Spaniards, Indians, and blacks who worked there but Mr. Hamilton and Mr. McKenzie, the autocrats of the mountains. Perhaps from delicate feelings McKenzie had left his concubines at home—whether his delicate feelings, or theirs, or those of the bereaved, Silk couldn't have said.

Srill, it was not an ideal audience. Though Mr. McKenzie was conspicuously dignified, Mr. Hamilton was on the verge of looking amused, and the *engagés* appeared to have had too much to drink.

It struck Silk as a shame that the only bereaved at the funeral, the only family, so to speak, was the one to preach the funeral sermon, himself. He lifted his voice into the spring twilight and brought forth:

Amazing grace, how sweet the sound

That saved a wretch like me
I once was lost, but now am found,
Was blind but now I see!

Since no one joined in with him—darned papists—Silk quit after one verse.

It did seem sad, Hairy being cut off untimely at the hands of the benighted redskins. Silk almost shed a tear—until he thought of his friend stretched out alive and smirking in the coffin at his feet. He wondered if the old boy was taking a snooze in there. Just to be sure, he thumped the box accidentally with one foot as he began to address the grief-stricken.

"Brethren," Silk began, "we are gathered here together to mourn the passing of our friend Ronald Smythe, rhymes with scythe, known to some as Shakespeare."

He raised his thin voice.

"Lord, we commend his spirit unto Thy bosom.

"Lord, we ask thy mercy upon his soul, that he may spend eternity in Thy everlasting arms."

Having begun thus formally, Silk spoke somewhat of Hairy's history, such as he knew it, trying not to offend by repeating the actor's fabrications. Silk then set off upon what he knew of his partner directly, and touched upon their meeting as the grizzly stalked the man, and Hairy's pity for the woman Iron Kettle, that led them to abide with the Crow nation, and Hairy outwitting the Cheyenne enemy. All this he described briefly but sentimentally, not including certain details that might have sullied the dignity of the moment.

He might have mentioned the pursuit of the horse thieves, but he thought a funeral sermon not an occasion for mirth. He would have spoken of Hairy's sojourn as an actor, and his skill with wigs and beards, but that might have called unnecessary attention to the element of deception. Besides, Silk observed that he was beginning to lose the attention of his audience.

Dramatically, Silk knelt beside the pine box. It must have seemed to the watchers that he looked at Hairy's wooden overcoat with tears in his eyes, experiencing a last moment of communion with his friend. In truth, he didn't know what he was going to say. And if he was going to say what had just come into his mind, Silk wanted to be close enough for Hairy to be sure to hear it.

"We confess, O Lord, that he was a man to try the boundaries of even Thy boundless patience. He played the fool on stage, Dear Jesus, until he became the clown in life. He pretended so often that he took himself in. And his judgment, Lord—why it was so shrewd that going along with him was surer than hanging. And his friendship—why, it was such that you were sure to be humbled, and usually humiliated."

Silk thought he saw the coffin actually move. Yeah, maybe it moved. The son of a gun was going to blow his disguise and get himself killed!

Silk rose, put a foot on the coffin, and leaned an elbow on his knee. Even McKenzie nearly smiled at this breech of decorum, but it couldn't be helped.

"But, Lord," Silk plunged on, "if he had the foolishness of a child, he had the sweetness as well. The innocence, Jesus, of a lamb. The affection, Lord, of a small daughter, and the playfulness of a little boy. To top all he had the luck of a drunk or a dimwit—surely, Lord, Thy angels must have been watching after him.

"He was a good man, Almighty Father, good enough to make you welcome him home. He cared for people and never hurt anyone. He was brave, brave unto taking terrible risks. He had a voice worthy of the thunder, Almighty God. He was loyal—a man could depend on him. He loved poetry and song, and saw poetry everywhere in life. And, Lord, he was filled with joy in the world You created—life around him was a barrel of fun."

Silk was beginning to touch even himself. He felt a tear threatening to well up. "The truth is, Lord, I didn't always know if I liked him." He blinked and the tear ran. "But I loved him, and I think You do, too.

"I'll miss him, Lord." He hesitated, looking down at the coffin. "It's not right for him to be gone yet."

Silk knelt over the box and cried unashamedly. He didn't know if his own tears were real or staged.

After a few moments McKenzie touched Silk on the shoulder. Silk stood up.

"If your men could just lower him," Silk said softly to the baron. McKenzie gestured and *engagés* moved to the ropes.

When the coffin was in the hole, Silk said, "I'd like to be with him a while yet. I'll shovel the dirt in myself." McKenzie motioned and everyone moved off.

Silk squatted by the open grave, a big black hole with Hairy at the bottom. He made a small, dark round shape above the blackness. The spade handle drew a thin, slanting line against the pearly sky.

Silk looked down at Hairy's wooden overcoat. There were still tears on his face. He whispered, "I did it, you sumbuck! We got away with it!"

The coffin didn't talk back.

23

take him for all in all,
I shall not look upon his like again

—Hamlet, I.i

S ilk poked his borrowed horse along beside the wash, heading for the spring. He and Hairy had found this spring, and a nice grove in a sheltered place, on the way to Fort Union. A good place to camp.

Silk was looking forward to eating big on the deer Hairy would have shot, lying about, and trading tales. Hairy would probably give a critique of Silk's funeral sermon, they'd remember together how Silk had pried the coffin lid off, Hairy would tell about nicking a pony out of the big fort herd, and altogether they'd celebrate the outwitting of McKenzie and the vengeful Cheyennes. And then they'd move on to that spot Hairy talked about, the white sulphur hot springs. They'd take a week there, Hairy said, just being lazy. Hot springs were a luxury, in Silk's eyes, big enough to get a man to take a bath.

Silk was proud of the tales he had to tell. It had gone off fine with McKenzie. Silk had buried the empty box, and spent three nights in the fort to make it look good. No, Mr. McKenzie, don't believe I'll accept employment. Yessir, I'm headed to Cass to meet my Crow friends. Yessir, I'd be pleased to take your letters along for fifty shinplasters. Nossir, I don't need to rest up a while longer. Yessir, I will be careful. All this, naturally, with a long face, an ineffable, world-weary sadness.

Sometimes it had been hard not to laugh.

It would be good to see Hairy, and to rest. And then to rejoin Jim and Pine Leaf and the Crows. And Rosie—Silk missed the doughty old mule.

There had been one bad moment with the baron. "Our reports have it," McKenzie ventured calculatingly, "that the Cheyennes mostly wanted Shakespeare, and not you."

"Probably," said Silk with a glare that added, "That's what they got, ain't it?"

"Our reports also have it that the Cheyennes are not in the country yet." McKenzie waited.

"You might not know," offered Silk.

"True enough. But let's say that some other Indians were guilty in this case. The Cheyennes may turn their vengeance toward you."

Silk hadn't thought of that. Great to get the devils off Hairy's tail. Not good to make them switch. Especially since Silk would lead them straight to the living Hairy. Whoa, hoss!

McKenzie asked the tale of the theft of the horse that wasn't Leg-in-the-Water's, and Silk gave it to him straight.

McKenzie pulled at his chin. "I shall send word to our Cheyenne friends that you were not responsible," he said, "and that the real culprit is dead."

With that he suddenly stood up, flashed his teeth, and nodded curtly. Leaving His Presence, Silk thought—that was the way of McKenzie, to make himself seem all-powerful, and you obliged to him.

As Silk went out the door, McKenzie added, "Still, I'd advise caution."

Silk snapped out of his reverie.

Magpies by the spring. Lots of them—carrion birds, they were. Silk urged the mare to a lope. Then she shied off and he had to dismount to get a close look.

A horse, with Hairy's hobbles on it. The magpies wouldn't leave even when Silk got close, the darned critters. Silk couldn't see how the horse was killed—maybe gutshot, since the birds had ripped that area open.

Silk knelt for a close look at…Yeah, that was the chestnut wig half pinned under the horse's neck.

Haire-e-e.

Silk backed off to where the mare was grazing. Hairy.

There was sign everywhere—hoof prints and moccasin tracks, but Silk didn't read sign well.

He sat down and put his head on his knees.

Why couldn't he cry now? He cried when it was fake, but he didn't have any tears now. He remembered the words he'd spoken over Hairy's coffin: "The truth is, Lord, I didn't always know if I liked him. But I loved him, and I think You do, too."

For a few minutes he sat there, head down, not really thinking. He remembered sometimes. Remembered when Hairy pulled him to the ground that night after they stood up to Fitzpatrick. Remembered when Hairy painted himself so crazy for the Cheyenne affair. Remembered when he and Hairy and Jim hugged, after the fight. And heard under those memories a stately, measured music with a high, poignant obligatto of loss.

In half an hour he was up and reaching for the reins. He knew what he had to do.

"Blackfoot," said Jim. "Not Cheyenne."

Pine Leaf, still on her horse, nodded. "Siksika," she hissed.

Yellow Foot got down and started checking out the ground more carefully. The horse was just bones now. Yellow Foot, with grief large in his soft eyes, picked up the chestnut wig and handed it to Silk.

It was Pine Leaf who found it. Hairy's finger. It had been hacked off, and now lay covered with sandy soil. It was the left-hand little one with the ruined walnut nail.

"Where's the rest of him?" Silk muttered.

So Jim explained that one sport of Blackfeet was dragging victims behind a horse until they died. Could be anywhere, any direction, within several miles. If it was close, the magpies would have marked it before.

This talk left everyone grim.

So the four of them looked the site over thoroughly and found, according to Jim, remarkably little. It had been a party of maybeso six or eight or ten men—hard to tell after all the walking around here, first by the men and then by the horses. A party out for ponies or scalps, looked like, from the light way they travelled. Came from the south—Crow or Cheyenne country—left to the north. Likely knew about this camping spot too, and just chanced on Hairy.

"I don' see his Shakespeare, either," Pine Leaf put in.

"No, they took their time and scavenged good," said Jim.

"What does a Blackfoot want with a book?" Silk asked, pouting. He'd hoped to keep the Shakespeare as a memento.

"End up at some trading post," Jim allowed. "Not close by."

He filled up with water, mounted, and led them off about half a mile, within sight of the spring but on higher ground. "Like Hairy shoulda done," he commented to Silk.

So they did the chores of making camp. Silk felt melancholy. He tried to think about his future. He would have to leave the Crows now, but had no partner. He could hunt for Fort Cass, probably—maybe he and Ginny would…Or he could go to rendezvous, and try to hook on with Rocky Mountain Fur. But hymns kept pushing these plans out his head. Hymns and memories.

Over a supper of pemmican he finally asked: "So do we go after them?"

Antelope Jim shook his head. "Trail's near three weeks cold now, and they were headed home. Have to hit the whole village."

"We hit Siksikas all times, all places," said Pine Leaf. "We take their blood. That's how they pay for Hairy."

"We'd never find them as done it," said Jim.

That flat statement sat between the four of them for a long moment.

"But if you want to follow trail," added Yellow Foot, "I go with you."

Silk shook his head. It was pointless. Seemed everything was pointless.

After dark he sat and blew hymn after hymn on the love flute, his own requiem for Hairy.

24

One fair daughter and no more

—Hamlet, II.ii

It was the talk of the fort: Ginny was gone. Kid-napped, it seemed.

Tulloch swung from brooding to raging. "Right out of her own home!" he would say suddenly and crash his fist on the table. "My daughter taken…" Then silence. Ginny's mother, the self-effacing Crow woman, said nothing but was not stoical—Silk saw her hauling water with tears on her face.

It was the Blackfeet apparently. A small band vis-ited the fort for several days while the Rotten Belly band was camped there and Jim, Pine Leaf, Yellow Foot, and Silk were gone to see about Hairy's death. Neutral ground or not, Tulloch had a bad time keep-ing the Crow outfit from rubbing those Blackfeet out. After a couple of days, Chief Rotten Belly led the Absaroka people off in a bad mood, unwilling even to be near the Siksikas.

Tulloch disliked and distrusted Blackfeet too, but this band had stopped to trade the previous fall, and the Blackfeet were being courted avidly by American Fur these days. So Tulloch really couldn't turn them away. The baron ordered, Get the trade at all costs!

The cost in this case was Ginny.

In all the hullabaloo Silk found out some about Ginny he didn't realize. She was an unusual breed girl—was born back in the U. S. somewhere and raised to be a real lady—had gone to Miss Somebody's finishing school and had high-falutin notions. Dead game, though, Jim said. Wouldn't stay back in the States like her dad wanted. Went with her adopted mother regular to live with the Pryor Mountain Crows. Treated Injuns like folks. *Negroes,* too—Jim caterpillared his lips as he said the word. She said she was an Abolitionist. Jim described that as an oh-so-generous organization of white people to give black people their freedom, which was already theirs for the taking. And Ginny could ride a horse agile and quick as a dust devil, and wouldn't have her head turned by nobody.

So Silk figured she must be some.

Tulloch kept fuming. He blamed himself for not being more suspicious. Why was that lot—small, but arrogant as any Blackfeet—this far south anyway? Yes, a stop to trade a few robes the previous autumn, that was understandable. Exploratory, probably, and Tulloch had instructions to barter generously. But why'd they come back? The new trading post, Fort

Piegan, was right in their back yard. Why, indeed, except to steal Ginny? His precious Ginny.

Why hadn't he let the Crows massacre them? Thus Tulloch sent up fumes and smoke, but would not erupt. Mostly he retreated to his ledgers.

He's a man who aims to live small, thought Silk. He's not going to do a darn thing. Ginny's gone (Silk already felt like her friend) but the sumbuck's gonna do nothing. Silk sniffed his contempt.

"What are we waiting for?" Silk challenged Jim. The big black was stoking his little clay pipe after dinner. He took time to light it and offer the pipe to the four directions, the earth, and the sky before he answered.

"Maybeso for daylight to start after Rotten Belly," Jim said evenly. But the gleam in his eye gave him away. They were camped just downriver from the fort. Rotten Belly had left word he would be hunting around the big bend of the Yellowstone, where he expected to find many buffalo.

"We got to get her," Silk said flatly.

Pine Leaf and Antelope looked at each other thoughtfully. Silk guessed they'd been talking about it. Yellow Foot just gnawed on more roast, their first fresh meat in five days. Yellow Foot seemed to eat twice as much as Jim, yet still looked slim and smooth-skinned as a girl.

"Antoine be here pretty soon," said Jim. Antoine was a breed who hunted for the fort. "That's what he's coming to talk about."

Jim puffed on his pipe quietly until Antoine slipped in out of the night and sat down without a word. He was young, fit, and good-looking, except for a hint of sneer. Silk felt mistrustful of him. Jim tapped out the pipe and refilled it and handed it to Antoine.

The breed took a hasty puff and raised his eyebrows at Jim. "You go?" he asked.

"Maybeso Ginny want to be with them," Pine Leaf offered. "Likes young warrior maybeso."

"Not that kind of girl," Jim said. "She's a real lady-lady."

"Besides, they're too ugly," Yellow Foot put in, grinning, and went back to eating.

"She wouldn't go off and not tell her parents and break their hearts," Silk added. He felt foolish.

Antoine eyed Silk strangely, then shook his head no. Turning to Pine Leaf, he said that if she was ever captured by the Siksikas, she would know why no woman should ever let herself be captured by those dogs. He snapped out curses on Blackfoot bodies and souls in three or four languages.

Antoine was so dark he might have been an Indian, except for the Frenchy accent in his English. The accent, which sounded sort of womanly, seemed queer coming from so fierce a face.

"And Ginny is Crow, hate Siksika," Antoine added.

"What you think?" Jim said to Pine Leaf.

"Better to have the Lumpwoods," she answered, meaning the men of that Crow warrior society.

Jim shrugged.

"I go," Antoine said. "Simple."

"Why not?" said Silk, a little irked.

So Jim, Pine Leaf, and Antoine spelled out the obstacles. The little band was headed north, maybeso anywhere into Blackfoot country, which was five hundred miles on a side. Being only three days old, the trail could be followed. Likely be easy to follow, in fact, and for that reason the girl would not be with the band. Some young men would be taking her another way—that trail likely hard to find, harder to follow. They'd be wary of being tracked from the fort. Worth a try, maybeso, but poor odds.

Antoine had an idea, though. For a couple or three weeks, the bands would be making the hunt of early summer. After that they would gather for the Sun Dance. Every bunch of Piegan and Kainah and Siksika from all over the north country would be there. Likely find out at Fort Piegan where the big doings were. Sure enough a place to spot the girl. Maybe tricky to march her off.

"We can't wait a month," Silk interjected.

Antoine shrugged. "Lots of riding good for a horse or a woman," he said with a malicious smile.

Silk felt himself flush.

Jim waited. Waiting to see if I do anything dumb, Silk thought. Antoine, I'll take care of you later.

"My problem here," Jim allowed, "is our army. This one"—he jerked his head at Pine Leaf—"is a soldier. Yellow Foot too. Antoine's an old hand. And you, Silk, are a gallant young recruit, but new to the game.

Such as might go on a war party to hold the horses and watch."

"I can fight," Silk growled.

So what was that icicle he felt inside? "Such kid endangers us all," Antoine said.

"Let me," Jim said to Antoine pointedly.

"Maybeso you can fight—for sure you can shoot," allowed Jim. "But we got a problem here. Goin' far, far into enemy country, we don't need no hotheads, no heroes, and no independent thinkers. There might be a way—just to get close and have a look-see, you cotton—but it has to be done easy and smart.

"This child don't start out till everyone understands they're soldiers and Antelope Jim is the general."

Antoine said of course. Silk agreed, louder. Pine Leaf lay back and looked at the stars. Yellow Foot grunted and kept eating.

"This child promises to hogtie you and lash you to the saddle if you get out of line," Jim said to Silk.

"I understand," Silk answered. He sounded scared even to himself.

Jim looked at him. "Believe you do. Actual, the general is more worried about you, Antoine."

"Me, my father, my grandfather all fight Siksikas," Antoine growled.

"That's how come I worry," Jim said. "You ain't scared, and you got reason. Besides, Tulloch says you been making eyes at Ginny for another wife. But you can't keep the belly of the wife you got full. Either of her bellies. Tulloch says I ain't supposed to let you close to his daughter."

Antoine said nothing, though his face looked full of words and feelings. Pine Leaf was watching Silk with a little smile.

"Wagh! This child tells you simple, Antoine. You get outa line and I shoot you. Backshoot, if I have to."

Antoine stood up and looked down at Jim. Finally he gave a little shrug. "First light," he murmured, and walked off into the darkness.

The four shook out their blankets and spread them. They'd talked until the big dipper showed about midnight, but Silk couldn't sleep. He stared at the night sky.

So. They were going to try to slip into an encampment of thousands of Blackfeet. They were going to try to ease Ginny out on the sly. And keep her away from Antoine.

A damsel in distress, and an antagonist for the lady's hand. But not fairy-tale stuff. Real as an icy knife-edge.

Silk blinked and turned the Milky Way into a grand smear. He made funny little sounds, sort of like chuckles, in his throat. He'd never been so excited in his life. Or was it scared?

25

where is any author in the world
Teaches such beauty as a woman's eye?
—Love's Labours Lost, IV.iii

S ilk held his glass on the girl. She was easy to pick
out in the village because her hair shone white as
Easter lilies in the sun.

No one had told him what she looked like. Ginny
Tulloch seemed about four-and-a-half feet tall. Maybe
four-and-three-quarters. She was like a doll—beautifully proportioned, erect of carriage, perfect as a porcelain figurine, outfitted in a showy skin dress glitter-
ing with German silver. But she was tiny. And at first
Silk thought she must be wearing a white scarf, but
she wasn't. Ginny, at seventeen, had rolled atop her
head abundant hair of dazzling white.

"The tow-headed one," Jim had said, passing the
glass. Silk would never have put that childish word to it.

"What gorgeous hair," he murmured. "Pure
white."

"Sort of," Jim said. "She's got it rolled in ermine tails. Actual hair is ginger. Makes it handy to spot her, don't it?"

Ermine tails—Silk liked that even better. Through the glass, Ginny was as a creature in a dream. Silk would give the rest of his life to her.

Jim tapped him and Silk handed the glass back. Antelope glassed the rest of the village. It was a circle of tipis spread comfortably around a big meadow on the south side of Two Medicine River, full of yapping dogs and shouting children. Ordinary and peacable as any village of Indians on these Western plains, except for two things: There was a score of other encampments just like it nearby, making a metropolis of enemies, and these Blackfeet were holding a white girl captive. The girl Silk had set his heart on.

She wasn't guarded. But why should she be— wasn't home several hundred miles away across enemy ground? What could a lone girl do in that spot? He looked around for the brave who stole her away. Though he'd spotted the tipi she slept in, he couldn't tell which man owned it. If it was a kindly older man who treated her like a daughter, fine. If a young man, a mate, Silk meant to have that man's life.

He didn't care about the risk. Jim would understand, when he thought on it.

Silk lay back in the cool of the crevice and relaxed. He and Jim were hiding in a vertical split in a sandstone bluff, not a mile from the village. The crevice was dark and cool. You could climb out frontways or straight up. "Snug as a bug in a rug," Jim said. Cool and concealed, anyway.

It had been a heck of a month. The five of them had ridden from the Yellowstone across to the Musselshell and over the mountains to the Judith and clear on north to the Missouri, near the mouth of the Marias. There they saw the charred remains of Fort Piegan, built the summer before to establish trade with the Blackfeet. When American Fur abandoned it for the winter, the Blackfeet burned the stockade down. A going-away present, Blackfoot-style.

But the little party of seekers heard about a new post just six miles on upriver, and rode over to talk to David Mitchell, the clerk of Fort McKenzie. Mitchell wouldn't tell them anything—didn't want outsiders messing around the Blackfoot Sun Dance. But the hired men at the fort said the Blackfoot get-together was up on the Two Medicine River, far to the west, in the shadows of the great mountains that divided the continent.

So the little band pushed its quest deeper yet into the land of the Blackfoot enemy. They rode by night and slept by day. When they passed the mouth of Cut Bank Creek, they searched for miles around until they found a concealed place to camp, in a dense grove in the bottom of a deep canyon, with graze for the horses and cover for the men. Were they not five against five thousand? That was when Jim asked Silk to come along and scout out the main camp and try to spot Ginny. Not to make any move, Jim cautioned, just to look-see. Silk thought maybe Antoine was miffed at being left behind, which was handsome. The two went off, wearing some of Pine Leaf's Blackfoot-style mocassins. They moved on foot and by dark.

Now they knew. Knew where Ginny was. Knew the layout of the camps and pony herds. Knew where the sun-dance ceremony itself was about to take place, led by a faithful woman. Knew what they had to know.

Silk asked Jim how they could manage it. The mulatto shook his head. "Silk," he said genially, "you can shoot. Sure can. Now you gonna learn the first skill of war. Waiting."

They lounged in the crevice all day, dozing off and on, watching the camp in its daily routine, trading riddles, mostly just waiting in silence. Silk imagined playing his love flute—the one Ginny had carved—to pass the time. Maybe it would entrance the girl magically, mesmerize her, lure her from the grip of the enemy to the arms of her lover.

That night Jim slipped out to walk the nearby hills, sneaking around to fix the lay of the land, he said, every hump and coulee, firm in his mind. The next day they lay in the crevice again and watched, deep in the shadows where the Blackfeet could not see and the sun would not catch the glint of the lens. Past midnight, in a thin rain, they moved out.

"No way," said Jim. "Get it through your head. You're staying with the horses."

Silk was popping with rage. The roots of his hair were afire. He sat back down, gasping for self-control.

Jim was sure enough playing the general. While they munched on pemmican, too cautious for a fire, he'd explained his plan. Himself, Pine Leaf, and Yellow Foot would slip around to the north side of valley—they at least looked like Injuns—and hide. Tomorrow night they would grab a Black-foot squaw from a village well away from Ginny's, take the clothes for Pine Leaf, then ease around to the crevice. The following evening, during the celebration before the scarifying in honor of the sun, Pine Leaf would move in disguised and sneak Ginny out.

No shooting, Jim emphasized. That's one reason they didn't need Silk. Nor did they need Antoine's hot head. The whole thing cool, sweet, and sly. Otherwise everyone could say goodbye to his hair.

If Silk didn't like it, Jim would offer him the alternative of being tied up and stuck in a tree again. Bound with something stronger than his sash.

Antoine sat flipping his knife into a log. He made no protest about his role. When Jim threatened Silk with tying up, Antoine grinned crookedly, and snicked the knife deep into the wood.

Silk kept his eyes down, away from Jim. It was midday. He had until maybe midnight to figure out what to do.

26

that one might read the book of fate
—Henry IV, Part 2, III.i

Still tense, Silk leaned over Antoine's crumpled form. He remembered to breathe out. It was over.

Silk had been lucky—it was easy. With Jim gone, Antoine tippled from his flask a little. Silk waited until the Frenchy was well along and conked him good with the rifle barrel. Had to make sure. Sumbuck needed conking anyway.

Silk didn't have a plan, but his aim was simple. The others were going to make a try to get Ginny two nights from now. Silk would do something tomorrow night.

James Pierson Beckwourth, mulatto son of an aristocratic Virginia slave-holder, lay back and enjoyed the night. He cast his eye around the dark sky, checked the time by the big dipper and the north star, and let his imagination play among the dark places on the moon a while. He had heard that these vast shadowy areas were great seas, and that big, barren mountains surrounded them. He didn't know. Men would never know. And Jim did not want to find out. He liked the idea that such a big hunk of territory was nearby, tantalizingly close to the eye, yet utterly inaccessible. Even to explorers like James P. Beckwourth.

He looked to the west, at Orion's starry sword and belt hanging there. He could remember nothing of what his dad had told him about the constellation except that Orion was some mythic hunter. Jim had felt the call of those stars, beckoning in the west, since he was a kid. And he had accepted their invitation, and was now himself a great hunter in the West. A mythic—by God!—hunter. If there were any Homers around to write big poems any more, Jim Beckwourth would be a whole damn poetic constellation.

He felt like having a pipe, but didn't want to disturb the woman lying against his chest. Pine Leaf, woman warrior of the Absaroka people, and his intended. They were stretched out on the buffalo robe he used for a saddle pad, and she was wrapped in a wool blanket. She would be sharing his robes and blankets for many a moon yet to come, and she would people his lodge with the bairns (to use one of Silk's funny words) of two mighty warriors.

She had whispered in his ear tonight that she meant to be in his lodge this winter, because she would bring forth a child in the Moon of Frost in the Tipi.

So he was contented. He'd always expected Pine Leaf to come to his lodge one day, and often thought their child would be the occasion.

How many moons they might share robes he could not say. He did not wonder about such things. He accepted fully the possibility that either of them might die tomorrow—may it be a good day to die! He accepted as easily the possibility that the world might have a new aspect next week, and he would have to follow his star to Californy or even the Sandwich Islands, or Pine Leaf follow hers likewise away from him.

Jim Beckwourth was not a man to live among prospects and speculations. He was pleased with the day.

And well pleased tonight. Pine Leaf was asleep on his shoulder, their friend Yellow Foot at his feet. Though they had no fire, and not much to eat, it was enough.

The nearness of their enemies the Blackfeet did not matter—the aspens were plenty cover. Tomorrow they would stay hidden during the day, and grab a Blackfoot woman in the place they'd scouted in the evening. A risk, but not a great one. The plan was for the woman to see only Pine Leaf, and her naked, so the woman wouldn't see the Crow clothes. And send the woman back to camp naked herself, keeping the clothes. A mystery it would seem to her men, but scarcely a threat.

And the next evening or two they would, or wouldn't, pluck Ginny Tulloch away from the

Blackfeet. It was given to Antelope not to see the future but to live gladly in the present.

In an hour he would wake Pine Leaf and make love with her once more. Her body was different from other women, so hard, like a man's, making him think of fighting instead of fornicating. But she warmed him. He could call from her what he'd seen her give no one else, a certain look. A glisteny softness, and fullness. When he first saw that look as he held her, more than two years ago, he had known she belonged to him.

He thought that look his biggest coup, too private and too precious to be spoken of.

Antelope Jim was contented.

Silk composed the message over and over. He was stuck down in the crevice until dark, and had nothing else to do. He wrote version after version in his head, putting flourishes into some. Finally he got out his notebook and stub of pencil and carefully lettered out the simplest version:

**HOSS—GINNY AND I ARE HEADED FOR
CAMP. WILL WAIT ONE DAY**

SILK

He laid the paper on the rock Jim was accustomed to sitting on, and weighted it with a fist-sized stone. Even in the dark, in the small hours of tomorrow morning, when they'd probably arrive, Antelope Jim might see the white paper. Surely he would at first light.

Now Silk only had one problem. He had no notion of how to spring Ginny.

And darn it, he couldn't even see where she was. Jim had the glass, borrowed for the purpose of working his own plan. If Silk had insisted on keeping the glass, Jim might have cottoned.

Silk was about equal parts agitated, excited, and frustrated. He rose up in the crack a little and eye-balled the village again. Maybe he could spot that sparkling white head, her heraldic emblem.

But they all looked like Indians to him.

Well, he'd think of something. He'd not Hamlet it, in Hairy's phrase. He'd slip in by dark and impro-vise. He'd use his advantage, surprise. Faint heart never won fair maiden.

Hadn't Hairy shown him, against those Chey-ennes, what one man can do? He squirmed back down into the bottom of the crevice. He ought to try to sleep. It was going to be some night.

Ginny stopped at the edge of the cedars. The sand-stone bluffs and the spy crevice were less than a hun-dred steps ahead. She turned and looked at the muscular young Blackfoot who stood near her. She felt quavery. He looked solemn and steady, his eyes deepset and shadowed beneath the hank of black hair that fell to his eyebrows.

She reached for his hand. He gave it, reluctantly. Holding his fingertips lightly, she looked around at the men of his warrior society, fully painted, fully armed, fully ready.

She knew they felt unsure of her. They trusted weapons more than wiles. She wondered if the man whose fingers she touched felt unsure as well. She hoped not.

She thought of the boy down in the crevice, spying. She had never met him, had only heard tell of him, and was taking a chance based on the tales. She wondered if she was doing the right thing.

And then smiled at feeling unsure herself, and stepped forward, her nearly five feet perfectly erect, and walked across the grass and the prickly pear and onto the sandstone bluff without looking back.

Bump.

He flicked at his chest.

Bump.

He brushed at his head.

Bump.

Silk woke up—woke up all of a sudden. Bump. Another pebble bounced off his lap.

He looked up into the wedge of late-afternoon sky above his head and saw the most amazing sight of his short life.

Ginny. Ginny Tulloch. Looking down at him and plinking him with tiny pebbles. And smiling.

Her ginger hair hung down as she leaned over the edge and the waning sun turned its edges into an aureole, a corona of gold tinged wth rose.

Her eyes were smiling.

Silk sat up and twisted to his feet. He started to climb up the side of the crevice and—and what?—touch her hand, embrace her, laugh and dance with Ginny Tulloch.

But she held him in place with a raised hand. Quickly and nimbly, tiny Ginny climbed down to Silk. She pressed both his hands in her small ones, truly beamed at him, and uttered her first words to him, "All this way for me." And squeezed his hands.

Her voice, he thought, was surprisingly low, an amber music, like the low register of a clarinet. Her face was a long oval, gorgeous, a miniature madonna's. Her eyes, Dresden blue and infinitely soft, held his.

She put a finger to her lips and folded herself onto a rock in front of him. Their knees were touching. "We must stay here till dark," she whispered, "or they'll see us."

"How'd you f-find me?" Silk stammered.

"Pure luck," Ginny said, and smiled mischievously. She just looked at him for a moment. "True luck," she added softly.

Silk's head swam. He understood Destiny.

"You're not alone?" she asked.

So Silk spoke of mundane matters, and not of the song in his heart—for that music he had no words. He told her about his scout with Jim, and the mission of Jim, Pine Leaf, and Yellow Foot to the far side of the great encampment. He recounted his lone bid to rescue her, not mentioning the shameful tricking of Antoine.

"Good friends," Ginny murmured. "They're coming here, tonight?"

Yes, to this very hiding place, Silk said. They could wait for their friends here, if Ginny would rather.

He told about the uproar at the fort, and the long trip across the plains to aid her. When that simple story was done, he told her about possessing the love flute she made. He could see in her eyes that she knew its music had enchanted the musician, Silk Jones.

When he asked about her kidnapping and her imprisonment by the Blackfeet, Ginny only shook her head and declined to speak of it. It must be agony, Silk supposed—she doesn't want to dwell on it.

Soon afternoon had turned to the long northern evening, and evening to a lucent, aquamarine twilight. They sat in sweet, tranquil silence. Ginny took Silk's hand and put her head on his shoulder and rested. Perhaps she even slept lightly. Silk sat still as ever he could. He watched the stars pinprick the amethyst sky and then grow bright, and let his mind meander among the flamingo-colored flowers of fantasy.

27

what charms,
What conjuration, and what mighty magic
                                        —Othello, I.iii.

The water was warm. It flowed soothingly down his body and eddied back and around and over him, gentling and lulling. His long hair was watercress—he rubbed it against his cheek and neck. A porcelain face looked out at him from a circle of milkwhite hair, and the irises in its large eyes were tiny goldfish.

Ginny grabbed his hand hard. She pushed against him with one arm and sat up, clutching his hand. Shadows. Dark blotches moving against the dark sky.

"Jim?" he whispered.

"Silk?" The voice was hesitant.

"It's me. And I've got Ginny with me."

The black man climbed lithely down, stepped onto a boulder and balanced there. He looked hard and direct at one, then the other. Pine Leaf and Yellow Foot came down deliberately.

Ginny separated herself from Silk. He could feel the difference in her across the space between them, as though her inner music had changed.

"Ginny," said Jim softly and firmly.

"Yes, Jim." There was a metallic edge in her whisper.

"Are we gone under?"

"I hope not."

"Surrounded?"

"Yes."

Silence. Silk could see the mulatto's face turned into his, and feel the dark eyes.

"Silk, I oughta scalp you myself," Beckwourth said hard. He clenched and unclenched his huge fist.

"Save Siksikas the trouble," rasped Pine Leaf.

"No. They promised." Ginny separated the words, like tapping them out. Amazing how hard she sounded now.

Pine Leaf snorted.

Yellow Foot was squatting shoulder to shoulder with Silk, and getting materials out of the pouch he kept around his neck.

"Hell, we're not even armed," Jim moaned. He clubbed his fist on his knee. They'd all left their rifles in camp as nuisances, and maybe dangerous temptations. The crevice was indefensible, a trap.

"We'll go at daylight," Jim said.

"Better now," said Ginny. "They wait, they'll get nervous."

"Daylight," repeated Jim. "They'll be less jumpy if they can see us."

Silk flinched, then shivered. Yellow Foot, having painted himself a little, was sending up a keening sound, a thin wail, all the more eerie for starting in Silk's ear.

Pine Leaf murmured in Crow to Jim and started painting herself as well.

"No need for death songs. Truly," Ginny said in a flat voice. Jim shrugged. Pine Leaf and Yellow Foot ignored her.

So Jim asked how the Blackfeet had caught on, and Silk was relieved to know that they hadn't just spotted him today—they knew Jim and Silk were here the whole time, and wanted to follow them back to their camp, but failed.

Pine Leaf joined Yellow Foot, singing her death song, an incantation that echoed hauntingly in the narrow, high crevice.

Jim talked it over with Ginny as if they weren't singing. The report of a black man and a white youth, she said, made it easy to figure. Her father had sent Beckwourth and his friend she'd never met. Just like her father, she said bitterly—boss you around, but let someone else do the work.

She appreciated, though, their crossing hundreds of miles of enemy country to help her. That was friendship, she said—misguided friendship. And she was sorry for her deceit this afternoon, she told Silk. She took advantage of his youth.

That hurt. Silk was fighting back tears. And Ginny probably was barely older than he was. He'd been so stupid.

The warriors had decided to watch the invaders and do nothing and follow them back to their companions—get the whole lot. But when Jim and Silk left in the small hours, the trackers lost them in the dark and the rain.

Ginny was surprised that only four had come. Brave people. Silk looked at Jim's face, but saw no flicker when the mulatto realized Ginny didn't know about Antoine.

"What are you not telling us, Ginny?" Jim asked sharply.

"You know what you need to know."

Silk thought she glanced sideways at him as she spoke.

Eventually the ululations died away, and the five sat a while in silence. As though the songs had kept him warm, Silk began to shiver.

At first light Jim stood up. "Let's do it," he said neutrally. He didn't whisper now, and his voice seemed to clang.

Ginny led the way, then Pine Leaf, Yellow Foot, Silk, and Jim—each one clambered up the wall of the crevice and stepped into the chill dawn.

In each of the four directions stood Blackfoot warriors silhouetted against the gray sky, tall, dark, and still.

28

I have no other but a woman's reason
—The Two Gentlemen of Verona, I.ii

So far so good.

Silk kept looking at Jim's face, struck by its impassivity. While the warriors circled them with bristling lances, marched them to camp roughly, and herded them into the council tipi, Jim's expression had been still as deep water. An enemy could read nothing there, certainly not fear.

Pine Leaf was so blank she looked bored. Yellow Foot kept his head down and still, as though in silent prayer.

Silk kept his mind on emulating them, and trying to figure what power let them hide their turmoil.

The lodge was huge, and Silk thought maybe even Black-feet wouldn't kill you in the council tipi.

As Silk sat down, a wave of dizziness swept over him. He wobbled, and caught himself with a hand.

He knew he showed sickly, and didn't care. He was going to die.

Silk forced his attention back to the head man, the one behind the fire pit. He was getting the ceremonial smoking started, lighting the pipe to make the circle of the men around the fire pit. Maybe that was good. But the crowd of young bucks behind, and women, scared Silk plenty. The young bucks looked to be steaming with bloodlust. And among the Blackfeet, Silk had heard, the women did the torturing.

Silk, he barked at himself—Shame! You're a goshdarn—no, a goddam—Judas goat. You've killed your friends! Enough self-pity!

Whether from fear or shame, he could feel the sweat run cold down his spine and down his crack and wet his buckskin pants.

When the pipe came to him, he puffed briefly, trying to look reverent, and passed it on. He knew he'd rushed it, but it felt like it would make him nauseous.

At last the talk started, in the Blackfoot language. Yellow Foot, next to Silk, whispered that the head man was asking why people of the Absaroka had come so far into Blackfoot lands. Then Jim told him (in words and signs) the simple truth, that they came to rescue Ginny, their friend.

When Jim finished, the head man said that his young men did not like the Absarokas here. They remembered all the crimes of the Absarokas against their fathers and mothers and brothers and sisters. They did not like to see Pine Leaf dressed in clothes stolen from a Blackfoot woman.

He paused ominously.

If the Absarokas came on a rescue mission, why did they bring a woman with them? Everyone knew Pine Leaf was a warrior, but they wanted to see what answer would be made.

"It is the way of Pine Leaf," Jim answered simply.

The head man pursed his lips, then nodded. "Let others speak," he said softly. He turned and motioned to someone in the back.

Ginny stood up in the crowd behind the circle of councilors and captives. Silk thrilled a little to see her. She had changed into a gorgeous blue blanket dress ornamented with elk's teeth. She waited a moment before speaking, her face flushed with reined-in excitement.

"My friends," she began in English, making signs at the same time, and looking at the captives. Her voice was firm and deep. Silk was proud of her. "I say friends because it was a gesture of friendship to risk your lives to save me. I have spoken to the people of the Blackfoot nation already and asked, since you came out of good will for me, that you be treated as my friends, and your lives spared.

"That, I hope, is what your captors must hear. This is what you need to hear: The Blackfoot people are now my people. I am here because I wish to be by the side of my husband."

Silk was sure he blanched. He thought maybe even Jim's face moved.

She motioned broadly with one arm to the man sitting by the door flap, in the position of least honor. He stood up.

"This man," said Ginny, "is…" Here she spoke a Blackfoot name Silk did not catch.

Silk glared at the young brave. He was tall and yet looked broad-shouldered. His entire face was painted blue. Across his forehead, clear to the bridge of his nose, hung a flat hank of black hair striped vertically with yellow. He wore a white-man shirt of heavy cotton, with German-silver arm bands. Between his hide leggings hung a full-length breechcloth of brilliant scarlet, elaborately quilled.

Sumbuck is dressed up to show off, grumbled Silk to himself. And he had to admit the effect was, well… magnificent.

"I carry his child," Ginny said simply, her face radiant.

"I have spoken of you as friends. And I have asked my brothers and sisters for your lives. Yet you are not true friends, because like my father, you do not understand me." She spoke decisively, Silk thought, boldly, even heroically.

"I address these words to you, and ask you to carry them to my father. It was foolish of you not to know that an educated woman, a lady, can love a Blackfoot man. Foolish and arrogant, in the way of the whites. You think yourselves superior to the people I have chosen for my own. You do not know them or me.

"My husband is a splendid man, his brethren a magnificent people. I am proud to be one of them, to have my son be one of them.

"Look with your own eyes and see my love. Hear me. Learn.

"Until your people change, we must be enemies. If necessary I would kill you, or my father, the grandfather of our child. For my love is the Blackfoot people and their way of life and the hoop of the people in which my son will grow to be a man." Her arm took in all those gathered in the council lodge, and in the village beyond, and in all the village that made up the sacred encampment.

"I believe that you came here in good faith. And I want you to carry my words to the man who calls himself my father. Let my people be."

Ginny and her husband sat down. Silk wished to hell she hadn't said that about killing them if necessary.

A man next to the chief began to speak, half audibly at first, casually. Yellow Foot's fingers said that he was asking why the Blackfoot should even talk of letting these captives go. They were Crows, barbarians, the authors of a thousand crimes past and future. A Blackfoot should not soil his eyes by looking upon a living Crow.

One by one the other councilors spoke their minds. All recalled the legion crimes of the Absarokas against The People, and some recounted the particular offenses of Antelope Jim and Pine Leaf. All talked briefly, in an offhand manner. What point, they seemed to be saying, could there be to debating the fate of Absaroka captives? Everyone knew what must be done with them.

Silk kept struggling for breath, and striving for control by reminding himself that he deserved what was coming.

At last the head man himself spoke again. He acknowledged the arguments of his councilors, so strong as to need no emphasis and brook no rebuttal. Yet he confessed himself moved by the pleas of Little Prairie Dog Woman, as he called Ginny. Maybe he was getting weak of will, to be swayed by a woman's tenderness. Yet he was.

Also, he said, he could see some small reasons to grant the captives life. It would be nice to think of these two fighters, Antelope Jim and Pine Leaf—what a boneless nation the Crows were, that a woman could be a war leader—in debt to the Blackfeet for life itself. For the rest of their days, at any moment of pleasure, such pleasure in living as a lowly Crow could find, they would have to think they owed this pleasure to the generosity of the Blackfeet.

Silk was thinking that he could tolerate dying—it was something anyone could do—if only he didn't have to be tortured.

Suddenly he wondered if he would have to see Jim and Pine Leaf and Yellow foot tortured. He heaved a little and was glad he had nothing inside to throw up.

Besides, the head man went on, it was funny to see the great woman warrior reduced to housewife garb. If the Absarokas were men, one of them would keep her so always, and big-bellied, and not permit a woman to fight their battles. Maybe one of the men of the

Blackfeet would want to keep her, and teach her to be a woman—would she not make a better Blackfoot woman than a Crow man? Pine Leaf's face was blank as ever.

Silk had a terrible thought. Had he not turned his thoughts away from Pine Leaf to a woman he'd never seen, had he remembered whose banner he swore to lift high, Pine Leaf would not be about to die. Silk Jones was a darned traitor.

The head man had another thought or two in favor of the captives: He admired the spirit of Absarokas who would come so far to rescue a friend, especially a friend who was not of their people. And he respected the courage of anyone who would come only four strong among the Blackfeet, outnumbered as the herds of buffalo outnumber the boys who scout them. But this was also Absaroka arrogance, so perhaps it should be punished.

He shrugged. He didn't know if they should live, his shoulders said—it was a matter of no great importance.

Perhaps, he said lightly, the young boy, the white-man Crow, could be allowed to take word back to the trader and the Crows, and the other three given the honor of dying bravely.

Silk felt a huge revulsion. He could barely keep himself from yelling out "No!" He was furious at the head man for angling toward that suggestion.

Suddenly a voice came from the rear—a woman's voice. Silk thought Yellow Foot's face almost showed feeling as he translated.

This woman, he whispered, was the woman of virtue chosen by the nation to lead the dance of the sun tomorrow. Her chastity spoke of the strength of the people, to be renewed once more tomorrow during the next sun.

The people should not be distracted by these captives on the eve of the great ceremony, she said. All minds should be turned to tomorrow, and to the sacrifices of the young men who would pay homage to the sun with their blood. Why not decide the fate of the captives on the day after? No one wanted to give these Crows any thought today, and certainly not tomorrow. Even Crows, if the ending of their lives started today, would not all be dead by morning.

Silk flinched at the hint about torture, and glanced at Yellow Foot's face in shame—and saw there what looked like a glint of hope. And then Silk thought of it: Two days of life may give Antoine time to spring us.

29

To one of woman born

—Macbeth, V.vii.

Silk wasn't gonna let it happen. He wasn't going back to the Crows all rosy-cheeked with his friends dead. And he wasn't gonna be no Blackfoot messenger boy.

He couldn't tell if his friends thought he would. When they came into this lodge under guard, Jim signed for no talking, even English. Silk tried to talk with his fingers, but Jim shook his head and made the sign for thinking. Silk couldn't say much with sign language anyway.

So he had to wonder what his friends were thinking, and figure how to let them and the Blackfeet know he didn't mean to live if Jim and Pine Leaf and Yellow Foot died. And maybe calculate how to get the best of the guard on the lodge once dark came. And keep his mind off whether Antoine would show up.

He took a long breath and let it out. It truly hurt to breathe.

Jim was sitting there, his face unmoving and mask-like in the half darkness. Pine Leaf lay with her head on his lap, the first time Silk had seen such an outward sign of intimacy. Yellow Foot had his eyes closed and face lifted to the smoke hole, as though praying.

Silk kept catching himself humming. Any old piece of any old tune, like as not hitched to another piece of a different tune in a way that made no sense. He swore he'd stop it, and heard himself humming as he swore.

How could he die with his friends? Better death, for sure, than dishonor.

He could stab himself. Maybe he could kill himself, or hurt himself too bad to travel. They'd taken his knife, but he had a piece of obsidian in the rat's nest of his shot pouch. That thing would shave peach fuzz. Yes, that would make a dandy cut. Course, it was too small to get in very far with. Might end up just scratching himself and being laughed at.

But he could cut his throat. It would do that slick. Nothing tough about a throat. Cuts easy, bleeds aplenty.

Silk braced himself to stop the swaying.

So. The picture of his own blood made him sick. He shook his head.

Silk wished he had the stuff of a hero. But he didn't—that was plain. He didn't. Sick at the picture of his own blood. He looked at that bit of awareness, like staring sober into a mirror.

Well, if he wasn't naturally a hero, maybe he could still act like one. That's what he would do.

He caught himself humming "Onward Christian Soldiers."

At least he hoped he'd act like one. When the time came.

If only Antoine could keep the time from coming.

Just then the lodge flap opened and someone stepped in from the bright sunlight outside. Ginny's young man, with a armload of something, which he laid down. Ginny followed with a big load, and set it down. As Silk's eyesight readjusted, he saw powder horns, bridles, blankets. Most of what they'd left at camp, but for the saddles and guns.

Silk reeled.

"Our young men found your camp," Ginny said faintly.

Antoine.

"What about Antoine?" Silk asked impulsively.

"He is feeding the magpies," she answered, eyes cast down.

First Hairy and now Antoine. Silk wondered if he was conscious yet when they found him, or still conked out. Was that Silk's fault too? Then Ginny spoke at Jim sharply. "You should have told them about him."

Jim shrugged.

"Red Bull wanted to help you," she went on, sounding angry. "Now he can't."

Jim paid her no mind.

"I'm doing what I still can for you," she said, and let it sit there. Silk readied himself. She nodded toward her husband. "We will come back in the dark, very late, and fix it with the guard, and save you from torture." Her eyes were dark with death.

She darted out the flap, and her man followed with measured step.

Silk heard roaring, as though from sea shells, in his ears.

Yellow Foot kept his face lifted, unchanged. Pine Leaf didn't stir on Jim's lap. Careful not to move her head, Jim started rummaging in the pile of goods. After a moment he came out with Silk's flute, and held it out to him.

Silk couldn't reach for it.

Jim smiled a light smile, easy and benevolent.

Silk took it.

"I'm sorry," Silk said.

No one answered, or acknowledged, or maybe noticed.

After a few moments, Pine Leaf said, "Silk, you should know that Antelope Jim and I are going to get married."

No more. Just that, flat and matter of fact. *Are going to.* Her style—run up the flag as the ship is sinking. And the way her scar made her lip pucker was very endearing.

So. The woman Silk carried a torch for belonged to his friend. Always had.

Silk Jones was growing up just in time to die.

Silk couldn't bring himself to play the flute. But a tune sang in his head, plaintive and beautiful:

I am a poor, wayfaring stranger,
A-traveling through this world of woe,
But there's no trouble, no toil or danger
In that bright land to which I go.
I'm going home to see my father.
I'm going home, no more to roam.
I'm just a-going over Jordan,
I'm just a-going over home.

30

If this be magic, let it be an art
—The Winter's Tale, V.iii.

They were sitting there in the dark, stiff and weary from hours of waiting, when the song came.

They had no plan, for they did not know how many men would come with Ginny and her man. Jim had told Silk to take care of Ginny himself, probably because she was small, like Silk. He had his piece of obsidian in his hand. "Be sure of her," Jim said. Silk would. It hurt to picture it.

So the Blackfeet would come to snuff out their candles, and they would fight—as the Blackfeet surely knew—and it would be over one way or another quickly.

Then they heard the song, softly on the night air.
Full fathom five thy father lies;
Of his bones are coral made:

The voice was unmistakable.
Those are pearls that were his eyes:
Nothing of him that doth fade,
But doth suffer a sea-change
Into something rich and strange.
Sea-nymphs hourly ring his knell:

Ding-dong.

Hark! now I hear them,—ding-dong, bell.
Silk felt Jim's hand on his arm, warm and firm.
Silk did not speak, but sang in his head: Shakespeare.
Shakespeare. They were going to live.

They moved at a trot through the moonlit night. Silk was uncomfortable at that pace on the rough-gaited horse, but kept pace without flagging. Beside him, grinning huge and fierce in the dark, was his partner Hairy, come like Lazarus from the dead.

It was magic, and so be it.

The big dipper said short of midnight—early in the northern night—so they had miles to go to the south. No time to talk yet. Just accept, and wonder.

Every bump on the strange horse hurt, reminding Silk that he was alive.

A couple of hours out Jim stopped to let the horses blow and talked quietly with Hairy's two Blackfoot companions. When the party rode on, the Indians turned back.

It was still dark when they hit the trail. It was a main trail, heavily traveled, leading to the Missouri River and Crow country—home.

Jim turned the wrong way on it urging his horse uphill, kicking it to a lope. Pine Leaf, Yellow Foot, Shakespeare, and Silk Jones followed as fast as they could go.

A couple of miles further, in a little valley, they stopped to let the horses drink. Silk asked Jim why they were headed the wrong way.

"They'll be after us. Already are. Not too many, because of the dance, but enough."

Jim took a deep breath. The sky was beginning to lighten. "This trail is too full of tracks for them to pick out ours. They'll figure we headed toward home. Fool 'em.

"Up ahead is Marias Pass. The west side of the mountains. The home of the Nez Percy and further on the fish Indians." He grinned. "The long way home. Might as well see a little of the country while we're here."

At mid-morning they laid up, well off the trail and deep in a thicket. Jim disappeared uphill with Silk's spyglass. And Shakespeare told how he came to be alive.

He held up his stump of a finger, leering at it. "This is what I got 'em with," he bragged. Pine Leaf and Yellow Foot were asleep, but Silk was much too excited.

"Got us, too," Silk complained with a smile.

"Sorry, lad. In the crucible of life and death, I didn't think of fooling you."

They had come on him in the last of the long northern twilight, just stood up suddenly around his campfire, perfectly silent. Four boys and a buck, Piegans. They motioned Hairy not to touch his guns, and walked into camp without even a bow raised.

Real solemn, they were, faces like death masks. The leader asked if the white man knew how to die bravely.

"That was where I got the idea," Shakespeare explained. "I told them I was braver than any of them. Told them I wanted to show them how to bear pain easy as birds bear the wind."

He handed Silk something strange from his shot pouch—a little ball made of many facets of mirror, on a thin gold chain.

Shakespeare took the ball back and held it up into the sunlight. It turned on the chain, throwing off glints of sunlight almost magically.

"Mesmerism," Hairy said. "This child can mesmerize you or himself or your mule, likely."

As Shakespeare told it, he lay down by his small fire while the Piegans watched curiously, suspended the ball from a stick above his head, and gazed into the reflected firelight while it twirled. He seemed to be mumbling to himself. Pretty soon he looked half asleep, though his eyes were still cracked open.

Hairy had his patch knife, wickedly sharp, in one hand. He held up the finger with the walnut nail. Then he began to make a thin cut around the middle section of bone. He did it calmly, slowly, even savoringly.

"You'd be surprised how little I felt," he told Silk. The pain was there, but small, like something at the wrong end of the spyglass.

"When I got to the bone, I kept right on cutting. After a while I handed them the piece of finger. They were right surprised.

"The buck asked kind of gruff if I could take my entire self apart like that for them, bit by bit. I smiled my ogre smile and told them I could. We just had firelight, so this child judged he could get away with it. Had the white wig with the scalp plug on. Ran my knife light around the plug and popped it right off and waved it for them to see."

Just then Jim walked back into camp. Pine Leaf and Yellow Foot both sat up suddenly. "No one," Jim squealed, squinching his nose. "Absolutely no one on our trail," he added. "We is home free. To the west." He pointed.

Pine Leaf lay back down and closed her eyes.

"So what big story was you spinning out?" Jim said to Hairy.

"I was telling the lad how I used my magical powers to become a chief among the Blackfeet," Shakespeare said.

"Wagh!" Jim shook his head. "Go right ahead. And tell us all how come you let us fret a whole day without letting us know you was close by with troops."

"Wagh!" exclaimed Shakespeare, like a whale spouting, "this child's feelings was hurt. My friends showed up half a thousand miles from home. I was going to introduce 'em to my new compadres and give 'em a dog feast. Then it turns out my friends never cared nothing to come after me. They was chasing some little gal. Didn't even think about their partner Shakespeare."

"If the Blackfeet are maybeso such good friends," said Pine Leaf with her eyes closed, "how come you don't stay with them?"

"Well," said Shakespeare, "I'm afeared to teach 'em mesmerism, and I've had so much fun teaching 'em three-card monte my welcome's getting thin."

He poked a thumb inside his shirt and brought out a grizzly-claw necklace, a really big one, with the claws separated by those fancy blue beads the Russians traded. And smiled his ogre smile at Silk.

"Wagh!" said Silk Jones. It sounded more like a squeak than a roar.

They stood beside their horses atop Marias Pass. They'd seen no sign of anyone on their trail all day.

"We can cross back to the east side in four sleeps," Jim Beckwourth said.

"Or we can go dally among the Flatheads or the Nez Perce," Shakespeare said. "Fine Injuns. Fine Injuns."

"Or we can go to Californy," put in Silk.

"I thought you were going to do big battle for me," Pine Leaf said.

"Well," said Silk, "I'll leave that to Antelope Jim."

"Sure am glad to see you, partner," Hairy said again.

Silk looked at him. "I come five hundred miles to get a fair maiden for my castle," Silk teased, "and what do I rescue instead? A fat, old man with a talent for mischief."

"One of many talents this child has," Shakespeare said amiably.

"Do me one favor, will you, Hairy?" Silk went on. "Don't get killed anymore? Please? Fake or real?"

"Ah, lad, don't you know?" said Hairy with an expansive smile. "Shakespeare's immortal." He reached over and bear-hugged Silk with one arm. "Immortal," he said softly in Silk's ear.